If Worms Had Machine Guns

(My Name is John)

A Novel

by

S. J. Daws

authorHOUSE®

AuthorHouse™
1663 Liberty Drive, Suite 200
Bloomington, IN 47403
www.authorhouse.com
Phone: 1-800-839-8640

First published by AuthorHouse   1/21/2008

ISBN: 978-1-4343-4511-0 (sc)

Library of Congress Control Number: 2007908304

Printed in the United States of America
Bloomington, Indiana

This book is printed on acid-free paper.

Jacket Design by Chris Kemp

This book is dedicated to
all who have faced seemingly insurmountable odds
and managed to somehow find their way back to the ones they love.

It is also dedicated to
those who patiently waited and prayed...
never giving up and never losing hope that someday, somehow,
the one they love would return to them.

May this book remind us of the incredible strength and resilience
of the human spirit,
and of the amazing power of love.
And may we always remember to 'keep the faith'.

Will someone please turn out the lights? Can't you see when a fellow is trying to sleep?

*I said will someone **please** turn out the lights?*

Even with my eyes closed I can tell it is too bright in here. I can tell I am not at home. Where am I? Wait...why can't I open my eyes? Why do I feel so strange? What is going on?

I will my eyes to open, and they do not respond. I will my arms to reach and feel my surroundings, and they do not respond. I will my legs to carry me out of here, and they do not respond.

My body feels numb. I sense there is pain, but I don't feel pain. What I feel is cold. It is freezing in here. Can someone please cover me with a blanket?

*Am I dreaming? If so, wake up! **Wake up now!***

Why am I so tired? Why is it so hard to think? My mind feels as if it is in a fog, as if it is trying to shut down. What is wrong with me? I am so tired. I just want to sleep.

Listen! Wake up! There are voices in the distance. Who is there? Concentrate! Try to make out what they are saying!

"Hurry, get Dr. Lewis! We are losing him! Has his family been notified? Does anyone know this man's name?"

My name is John.

The Birthday

"We have a heartbeat. He's back with us for now."

"His name is John David Hughes. He is forty-nine years old."

"Has the family been contacted?"

"Yes."

"They need to get here a.s.a.p."

What do you mean we have a heartbeat? He's back with us for now? Has the family been contacted? What in the world is going on here?

Ok, it is finally starting to come to me. Think, John, think! The birthday, the dinner, the car...

It had been a good year. The real estate market was booming. We were having a record profit year in our business. The two older boys were out of college, and I had been able to pay the house off and become debt-free. Our savings account was growing and I had been able to set aside a nice start to our retirement.

Nikki had mentioned wanting a new car, but I hadn't given it much thought since hers was not giving us any trouble. That is, not until the week before, when we had passed a Jaguar dealership while we were out for a drive.

"Did you see that?" There was excitement in her voice.

"See what?"

"That car!"

Nikki's fiftieth birthday was a week away, and I hadn't seen her excited about anything lately. No, she wasn't happy about turning fifty, and she didn't want to talk about it. "Fifty, that's ancient," she had said. And she made me promise there would be no surprises and for sure, no party. She made it clear that this was nothing to celebrate, and I knew she meant it.

I turned around and headed back to see what had gotten her attention. We pulled into the car lot, and there sitting in the showroom was a Jaguar S luxury sedan. We parked the car and walked over to get a closer look. It was ebony black with champagne leather interior.

"John, isn't it beautiful?" she asked.

"Dream on," I said as I looked at the sixty grand sticker price.

"Yea, in my dreams," she sighed.

The next morning I was up early and had gotten to work before Rick. As soon as he had walked in, I told him to come with me, that we were going to take a drive. Rick had been my best friend since the summer before the eleventh grade. We had been through college together and had become partners in a real estate company soon after graduation.

We drove to the Jaguar dealership and I pulled up as close as I could. "You see that car?" I asked as I pointed to the showroom.

"Sweet!" he whistled.

"I am going to buy that car for Nikki's fiftieth birthday."

We spent that entire workday making plans. I would take Nikki out to a nice dinner that Friday night. Rick would move our car while we were inside the restaurant and replace it with the new Jag. The salesman had promised to have it ready for Rick, shining more than a car had ever shined before and topped with a big red bow.

"Oh, come on, Nikki, lighten up," I had joked. "I say, given the alternative, I will take the birthday."

"Very funny," she said, far from amused.

"I tell you what… I will make reservations for Friday night at the Lake, something very low key, just you and me. We will have a nice dinner and we can make plans with the boys over the weekend to maybe grill out or something. Doesn't that sound good?"

"Fifty, John!"

"I know. Hey, I am right behind you." Nikki was six months older and I had always enjoyed teasing her that no matter how old I got, she would always be the older, but this was certainly not the time for teasing. "So, can I make the reservation?"

"If you must."

We loved eating at the Lake. The food was delicious and the view overlooking the water was beautiful. I called the restaurant and reserved a special table in the private dining room and called a florist to have a flower arrangement sent to arrive ahead of us. I had instructed them to make something special and to make sure it was colorful and cheerful.

"You make fifty look beautiful, Nikki," I told her as I pulled out her chair. It was good to see her smile. She had surprised me by waking up in a good mood that morning. "The flowers are beautiful," she said.

I ordered the steak and Nikki ordered the shrimp. We had a Caesar salad and talked about the boys and how good it would be to have everyone together the following night for the cookout.

"I think I will grill some ribs," I said. "That is David's and Chris' favorite. And throw on some chicken for Charlie."

We hadn't seen much out of David lately. He was busy with his career and his new role as father. I was excited about us all being together.

"Don't you think I look too young to be a grandmother?"

"Definitely! And I look too young to be a grandfather." We laughed.

The waiter came and refilled our glasses and asked if we wanted any dessert.

"No, thank you," Nikki said.

"Oh, come on, Nikki, let's live dangerously." We ordered a brownie bottom pie, my favorite…a warm, rich, gooey, chocolate brownie covered with vanilla ice cream and caramel syrup and whipping cream and nuts with a cherry on top. Pure heaven!

"Just bring one," I had told the waiter. The portions were huge, and I knew Nikki would only take a couple of bites.

I reached in the pocket of my jacket and took out her birthday card and handed it to her.

She read aloud the words I had written inside. "Happy Birthday, Nikki. Thank you so much for my three precious boys. We have been through a lot, but we made it. I hope this is your best year yet. I love you! John."

She smiled and took my hand.

"John, you have put up with so much. No one could have blamed you if you had given up on us. I couldn't have asked for a better dad for our boys. Those times when I was emotionally shut down, you always picked up the slack and made sure they had what they needed. When you left, and I thought I had lost you for good, I finally realized what you had been trying to tell me all those years. Oh, John, if I could do it all over again, I would do it so differently. I hope you know that."

In all our years together, Nikki had never talked about this before. I sat quietly and listened as she continued.

"John, the day Daddy died, I heard you tell him you loved me and would always take care of me. I realized that day what a fool I had been. I decided then that I would quit making everyone miserable and be thankful for my blessings and enjoy each day with you and our boys. I regret all those years that we missed, John, but I am thankful we have now. You are such a good man. I am so sorry for all those times I wasn't there for you and for our boys."

"That is all in the past, Nikki. Everything is okay now." I could tell she meant every word. I knew what she was trying to say. Life with Nikki had been a challenge, to say the least. And yes, many times I had wanted to hit the road. But here we were. Yes, we had been through a lot, but we had made it.

I leaned over the table and kissed my wife on her birthday and ate the dessert until the very last bite was gone. It was hard to contain my excitement thinking of the surprise waiting for her.

We walked outside toward where we had parked the car. Nikki suddenly stopped. "John, I could have sworn we parked here. Our car is gone."

She looked around the parking lot and saw a brand new shiny, black Jaguar with a big red bow on top. "Hey, isn't that the car we saw the other day? Look, it has a bow on top. Some lucky dog has quite a gift over there."

I pulled the keys out of my pocket. "Happy birthday, you lucky dog!"

"It's mine?" she squealed with excitement.

"She's all yours!"

"Oh John, I love you!"

"You drive," I said, handing her the keys. "See how she feels."

The last thing I remember is that big smile on Nikki's face. It was good to see her smile. It was good to see her happy.

Wait, there's more. Something went wrong. Something went terribly wrong.

My wife...Where is my wife?

She's Gone

"Chris, meet me at Memorial Hospital."

"What's wrong, David?"

"It's Mom and Dad. There's been an accident."

Rick paced nervously. He walked down the hall to the doors leading to ICU. He looked inside the glass to see if anyone was coming. He walked back up the hall to the waiting area where he had told David to meet him. He felt like he was losing it. He couldn't get the image out of his head. He couldn't quit seeing the crash site he had driven up on and the new black Jag smashed in and turned sideways in the middle of the street. He had pulled over and had run toward the crowd that had gathered. A police officer was already on the scene, and the sounds of sirens were screaming in the distance.

"Oh, God...No!" He tried to push through. The policeman had grabbed his arm and told him to step back.

"I saw the whole thing," a guy was telling the officer. "See that kid walking around over there? He lost control of his car and came over into their lane. He crashed right into the driver's door. I was the first one there. The kid got out and I asked him if he was alright. He said he was. I got closer and could smell the alcohol. He's going to be fine. Isn't that the way it always is? I can't say the same for that poor couple. The woman was killed instantly. She never knew what hit her. She was already gone when I got to her. That man is messed up bad. He's probably not going to make it."

"You can't go over there," the officer told him as he tried again to push his way closer.

"You don't understand. I know them. That is my best friend. Please, I need to get to him."

"The ambulance is here. Everyone back!" the officer yelled.

Rick had followed the ambulance to the hospital and had called David on the way. When David had asked how bad it was, Rick had lied and said he didn't know, just for him to get there as fast as he could. David said he would call Chris and would be on his way.

He looked at his watch and knew the boys would be there any minute. There wasn't a man alive who loved his boys like John did, and Rick knew he had to pull himself together. John would expect that. John would do it for him. He knew this was going to be the hardest thing he had ever done.

"David, over here."

"Rick, where are Mom and Dad?"

"The doctor is with your dad right now, David. He will be out soon to let us know what's going on in there. Where is Chris?"

"He's on the way.

"Rick, what about mom?"

"Linda has gone to get Charlie and bring him here. He was staying over at a friend's house tonight."

"Rick, what about mom?"

"There's Chris. Over here, Chris. Let's talk over there while we wait on the doctor."

"You know your dad took your mom out for a birthday dinner tonight. There was an accident after they left the restaurant."

"How bad was it?" David knew the answer to that question before he asked. He could see the sadness and fear in Rick's eyes. He could hear the emotion in his voice as he struggled to find the words he needed to say. He wiped a tear away and continued.

"It was bad, David. Your dad had a surprise for your mom tonight. He had bought a new Jaguar for her birthday. He was going to surprise you boys and show it to you tomorrow night at the cookout."

"No way," Chris said, temporarily distracted by the thought of his dad buying something he would call insanely frivolous. "That is so out of character for Dad."

"Yea, I left the restaurant about five minutes after they did. You see, I had switched the cars for John while they were dining." Rick was trying to stay strong as he talked, but he was falling apart inside. He was stalling, trying to figure out how to tell them their mom was gone and their dad was lying in there fighting for his life.

"Rick, what about Mom?" David asked for a third time.

"Guys, I am so sorry. There is no easy way to say this. They were leaving the restaurant headed home. Your mom was driving and someone came over into their lane and hit them. Your mom…she didn't make it."

David and Chris were trying to process what they had just been told. They held on to each other and began to cry. The crying turned into deep sobbing. "No, Mom can't be gone!" Chris wailed. "It's her birthday!"

"They said the kid driving the car that hit them was leaning over the seat. They figure he was messing with a cell phone or maybe changing the music in his stereo. He had been drinking and they said driving way too fast. He lost control. He's going to be fine. Isn't that the way it always is?" The comments at the accident scene kept playing in Rick's head. He again saw the image of John's lifeless body as they loaded him in the ambulance. He knew John would want him to be there for his boys, but he just wanted to go somewhere and yell at the top of his lungs, "This isn't fair! How could something so senseless happen?" The words were screaming inside his head. Rick grabbed the boys and hugged them. His legs went limp and he got dizzy and felt like he was going down. He steadied himself.

"Rick, is Dad alive?" Chris stopped crying and turned to face Rick as David's question echoed through the room.

Rick's face drained of all its color. "It was a bad wreck, guys. Your dad is in bad shape."

"Here comes the doctor."

"Are you the John Hughes family?"

Shock was setting in, but somehow David managed to speak. "Yes, I am his son, David, and this is his son, Chris."

"I am Dr. Lewis. I have been the attending physician since your father was brought in. You are aware there was a car accident. Have you been given information concerning your mother?"

"Dr. Lewis, I am Rick Jones. I am John's business partner and friend of the family. I have told them about their mother. How is John?"

"I am so sorry for your loss. Let's go into the family room so we can talk about your father." Dr. Lewis motioned for everyone to sit down. "I know you want to see your father, but there are some things we need to discuss first. Your father has suffered severe head trauma. When he first came in, he wasn't breathing on his own. He is stabilized for now, but his condition is very serious."

Dr. Lewis looked down at the chart in his hand and paused for a long while. He continued, "I will let you go in to see him, but it will have to be a very short visit. You need to be aware of his situation and prepare yourself for what you will see when you go into his room in ICU. Your father is unconscious and is hooked up to wires and tubes and machines. These are needed to monitor his vital signs and oxygen saturation levels. IV pumps are providing fluids and medications, and with your father's head injury, it is imperative that we have a continuous reading of the fluid pressure on his brain. You will see your father on a ventilator. Now, I told you he wasn't breathing when he was first brought in, but before we hooked him up to the machine, he was breathing on his own. That is a good sign. We want the ventilator to breathe for him for awhile. That will take stress off his body and allow him to conserve much needed energy.

"I am going to check on my patient, and if you will wait here, I will have a nurse come for you when you can see him. Again, let me caution you to plan for a very short visit. Do you have any questions?"

There was silence. Dr. Lewis turned to walk away. He had learned a long time ago he had to stay emotionally detached, especially working in ICU, but his heart ached for David and Chris and what they were going through. He thought of his own sons and knew when he got home he would hug them and tell them how much he loved them.

"Is Dad going to make it?"

Dr. Lewis stopped and turned around. "I can't answer that, Chris. Your father is in critical condition. For now, let's see if we can get him through the night."

My Boys

$\mathcal{R}$ick continued to pace. He looked down at his watch again. It had only been a minute since Dr. Lewis had left them, but it seemed like hours. He wondered if Linda and Charlie were on the way. He looked over at David, who sat motionless, slumped over in a chair. A steady stream of tears was running down David's face. He looked over at Chris, who sat with his head down and his eyes closed.

Chris suddenly jumped up and walked to the door and looked down the hall. "I thought we could go see Dad."

Rick looked at his watch once again. "It hasn't been but a couple of minutes, Chris. The nurse will be here soon to get you. I wonder if Linda and Charlie are on the way."

"Charlie." David straightened up. He reached for a tissue on the table next to his chair and wiped the tears from his face. "Charlie will be here soon," David thought aloud.

"The nurse is coming." Chris walked toward her as he talked. David got up and walked behind him, then stopped and turned toward Rick.

Rick motioned for him to go. "I will wait here for Charlie. Go see your dad."

They walked down the hall to the two large wooden doors labeled ICU. The nurse pushed them open and David and Chris followed close behind. They walked past the nurses' station and down another hall. They passed three closed doors. The fourth was open, and they walked past family members standing in the hall, some of them crying, while doctors and nurses worked on the man inside. The nurse stopped at the fifth door and opened it. She motioned for David and Chris to go inside.

They walked slowly through the door. Dr. Lewis had told them exactly what to expect, but there was no way they could have been prepared for this. They walked to the bed. David went to the right side and Chris to the left. They stood there for what seemed like an eternity…staring down at the man in the bed. Their dad was a big, strong man. He had always been larger than life. Now he lay there looking so helpless, so frail. They noticed his chest moving up and down and followed the tubes over to the machine forcing air into his lungs. They looked around at the other machines and at all the numbers flashing on the monitors and the IV quietly beeping as the medicine dripped into his arm. David started to feel sick on his stomach when he saw the wires imbedded into his father's head. He looked closer at the stitches down the right side of his face, and the cuts and bruises down his right arm. David reached for his father's hand and gently wrapped his hand around it. "I'm here, Dad."

Chris took his left hand. "I'm here, too, Dad." The tears started to flow once again.

My boys! My precious boys! Don't cry, Chris. It's alright, Son.

"Is everything okay in here?" A nurse had come in to check the IV. She was a different nurse from the one earlier.

"Can Dad hear us?" David asked. "Does he know we are here?"

"Probably not." Her voice was sweet and reassuring. "But you never know. Each patient is different."

I can hear you, Boys! Don't be scared. Dad's here!

No man has ever been more blessed. It seemed like only yesterday that they were babies and I was rocking them to sleep, and only yesterday when David learned about monsters and Chris was afraid of the dark. I would go in their room and lie down with them and tell them not to be scared, that Dad was there. It always made everything alright. Now here they were all grown, David with his own family, and Chris engaged to be married.

It always amazed me how two boys could have the same parents and be raised in the exact same environment, yet be so different. These two were always as different as night and day. But that kept life interesting. I couldn't put into words how proud I was of both of them, and the men they had grown up to be.

John David Hughes, III...my first born son. David was not planned. We were still in high school when we found out Nikki was pregnant. I was young and scared, but once David was born, everything about my life seemed to finally make sense. He was as much like his father as a son could be. When he was six years old he had come in while I was working on taxes, and after questioning me for half an hour about what I was doing and why, began to stress over whether he would know how to do his taxes when he grew up. I knew then that he was a chip off the ole block. I had worried about such things at his age...things that other kids didn't have a care in the world about.

David studied hard and I never had to tell him to do his homework. He made good grades and the teachers loved him. He was always polite and well-mannered and their favorite kid in class.

The day he got his driver's license, he went down to the service station where I bought my gas and talked Mr. Cole, the old man who owned the place, into hiring him to work on Saturdays. When school was out that year, Mr. Cole hired him on full time for the summer. One day I had pulled up for gas and asked him how my boy was doing. Mr. Cole had spit the tobacco juice in his mouth into a cup and said, "John, that boy is pure gold. He works hard and you wouldn't believe the girls lined up at the full service pumps to have him put gas in their car. Yep, that boy is good for business."

David was tall and had dark hair and brown eyes and an athletic build. And Mr. Cole was right; the girls liked being around him, and not just because of his good looks. He had a way of making everyone feel special. But there was only one girl for David...his high school sweetheart, Jessica.

He came to me after working that first summer at the station with his plan in place. He surprised me by showing me two thousand dollars he had already saved. He wanted to put it down on a red mustang he had seen for sale. David had already taken a mechanic over to check it out. He told me if I would take out the loan for him, he would make the payments and would pay for his insurance. I put a thousand dollars down on the car along with the two thousand he had saved, and took out a loan for the rest. David never missed a payment. He kept that mustang washed and waxed and full of gas from the money he made at the station.

That is the way David approached life. He made a plan and did what he had to do to make it happen. He got a full academic scholarship all four years of college, graduated with honors, got his law degree, passed the bar exam, married Jessica, and at the age of thirty-one, had just become a father. He and Jessica had a baby girl and named her Allison.

What a little angel! I remember the feeling I had when I saw my first born son holding his little girl for the first time and saw the pride and joy in his eyes. "Dad, what in the world do I know about raising a little girl?" he had asked. "Just love her, Son," I had answered. I knew that being a father would be the most natural thing in the world for David.

He had spent some time working as a public defender, and had just recently been hired to work with a private law firm in the city. You could look at David and immediately know he was my son. "He looks just like you spit him out," old Mr. Cole at the station would say. We had always been close and he had always felt comfortable talking to me about anything and everything. My father had died when I was a teenager, and I had missed having that relationship with him as an adult. It was great to have that with David. I would always be his father and he would always be my first-born son, but we were also very good friends.

They say there is balance in life. I tend to believe that, because four years later, along came Chris...Christopher Walker Hughes, my wild child. Whereas David was serious-minded, motivated, and disciplined, Chris was just the opposite. He was the jokester, always finding humor in any situation, whether appropriate or not. He was fun-loving and care-free and a teacher's worst nightmare. Chris saw no need in education. He saw school as a total waste of his time. And more teachers than not thought his pranks and clowning in class were less than amusing.

Chris had been a short, chubby kid and the poster boy for laziness. He loved to eat, sleep, watch TV, play video games and stay up late. It took an act of Congress to get him up each morning, and we had more battles over his homework than I care to recall.

He had his mom's blonde hair and blue eyes, and in the ninth grade something happened to my boy. He came to the breakfast table one morning and there sat this kid who had thinned down and grown tall and cared that his hair was combed for school. I thought that was a good thing until I realized he had decided girls were cool. Yes, Chris liked the girls, and he was attracted to the ones you wouldn't necessarily bring home to 'Mama'. If she had very little clothing on with a navel ring and other piercings, then so much the better as far as he was concerned. No father has had as many talks with a son as I had with Chris. I would talk to him about love and life and school and grades and the importance of preparing for his future. But mainly, I talked to him about dating and girls and protecting himself and how all of life's choices had consequences. And as with everything else, Chris managed to take a serious discussion and make light of it. "Dad, lighten up," he would say. "I am young; I am supposed to be having a good time." And that is just what he did. No matter how frustrated I would get with Chris, he always managed to turn any situation around and make me laugh.

The day he graduated from high school was one of great relief. I knew he would get to college and party instead of go to class, but I insisted he go that first year anyway. He had a great time and spent my money and failed most of his classes, so I figured it was time for Mr. Christopher to see what it was like in the real world.

He had gone from job to job and from girl to girl. Who would have known that on David's wedding day, Chris is the one who would have the biggest change in life? That is the day he met Paige. Paige was Jessica's cousin and one of her bridesmaids. She was as cute as could be and had the sweetest smile you ever saw. She had no piercings and was just the type girl you would take home to 'Mama'. And to top it off, she thought Chris was funny. She laughed at his jokes and they hit it off immediately. They were inseparable after that day. Chris found his direction and motivation in life that day in a sweet heart named Paige. He went back to college and got his degree in Business and Finance and got a job selling insurance. He had been the top salesman in his region that year, and his 'gift of gab' had finally been put to good use. I don't know about selling ice to the Eskimos, but that boy could sure sell some life insurance. He had given Paige a ring this past Christmas and at twenty-seven, my son's life was finally headed in the right direction.

I am so proud of you boys. I love you so much!

"You can see him for a few minutes." David and Chris turned around as the nurse spoke. There stood Charlie in the doorway. His face was red and his eyes swollen and David went to him and hugged him. He kept his arm around Charlie as they walked toward the bed.

Charlie was shaking. "Dad, open your eyes." He looked around the room. He looked at all the machines and tubes and wires. He looked over at Chris. He leaned over the bed and gently put his head on his dad's chest.

My baby boy, Charlie... You are here, too.

Charles Brandon Hughes...my youngest son, Charlie. He had not been in my plans, either. David and Chris were twelve and sixteen and I was still going to be a young man when my boys were grown and gone. I liked the sound of that. "You have your kids while you are young." Good advice, I thought.

As far as I was concerned, my family had been complete for a long time with the two boys. There were a lot of things going on in my life during that time, and Nikki and I were not getting along at all. We had even separated for the first time in our rocky marriage, so another child was the farthest thing from my mind. Nikki, however, had other plans.

When she told me she was pregnant again, I had a lot to deal with and there were some important decisions to be made. But bottom line…Charlie was my boy, and he didn't ask to be born, and he deserved his dad being there for him just as much as David and Chris had.

Charlie was fifteen now, and I couldn't imagine my life without him. He had been a great little kid, full of energy. He kept me on my toes at all times. It turned out to be easier raising him with some age and experience on my side. I wasn't so uptight about everything, and I knew after raising Chris, that no matter what you encountered, you do the best you can, and with a little luck and a lot of prayers, things can turn out okay. I learned to just relax and enjoy the ride.

Charlie was my basketball player. He had been interested in having a ball in his hand from the time he was old enough to hold one. 'Ball' was the first word he ever spoke. I set up a goal in his room when he was three, and we continuously heard the steady thumps and thuds coming from his room as he played for hours.

He went through one period of liking girls, but that was when he was in pre-school. There was this little girl in his class, and he was fascinated with her bright red hair. He would come home from school and tell me he couldn't wait to grow up so he could marry her. He even got in trouble one day for kissing her right there in front of everyone during story time.

Thankfully, girls were out of the picture for now and basketball was his only love. Charlie made decent grades, but his main focus was playing the game he loved. I was glad he didn't stress out over his grades as David and I had done, and it was nice not to have to worry about his grades as I had done with Chris. Charlie seemed to have found that perfect balance with his classes and with the sport he loved.

Charlie had brown hair and green eyes and looked a lot like Nikki's father. David and I were 6'2"; Chris was 6'1". Charlie was tall and thin and had the perfect build for a basketball player. He was already 6'2" at fifteen, and the doctors had projected a possible height of 6'5" to 6'7".

His coach had moved him up to the high school team early and a couple of colleges had already started keeping an eye on him. He was fast and coordinated and could play defense and could sink a basket from way behind the three point line. I was always the proudest dad at every game.

That's my boy!

The nurse came in and looked at the blood pressure readings and checked the IV. "I'm sorry, but visiting time is over."

Charlie raised his head off his dad's chest. "I want to see Mom." Chris looked up at Charlie. "Tell me she's alive, Chris. Tell me Rick made a mistake. Tell me Mom is alive." Chris quickly looked back down.

"Please don't die, too, DAD! Dad, can you hear me? Please don't die, too."

David hugged Charlie again and tried to walk him toward the door. "No, I am not leaving him."

"Come on, Charlie. Dad needs his rest. We need to talk."

"Please let me stay," Chris begged the nurse. "I promise to be quiet."

"I'm sorry, but I've let you stay longer than I was supposed to. Why don't you try to get some sleep? It's late and you can see your dad again in the morning. You will be notified if there is any change."

Hey, they don't have to leave. My boys can stay here with me. Can't you see they are upset? Can't you see they need their dad?

What did Charlie say? Tell me Mom is alive? Don't die, too, Dad? What's going on here? Why am I so tired? I wish things made more sense.

Oh, no...please, no! That's what I have been trying to remember...the car coming toward us, yelling at Nikki to look out, the sound of the crash....NO, NIKKI, NO!

I don't feel so good. I need to sleep. Stay awake, John. The boys need you. So tired...Yes, David...Need to rest...Nikki... No, Not Nikki...So very...tired...

Call in the Family

"How long have I been asleep?" David got up from the recliner and stretched. He folded the blanket the nurse had brought him the night before and put it on the table in the corner of the family room.

"You've been out a couple of hours."

"Did you get any sleep?"

"Not really."

"Where are Chris and Charlie?"

"They went downstairs to get some breakfast. I told them to bring us some coffee."

"Coffee will be good. I wonder when we can see Dad."

Rick looked at his watch. "It is almost six-thirty."

David's head hurt. He wanted to avoid the subject, but knew he needed to talk to Rick while his brothers were gone. "Listen, Rick, I know we have to make arrangements for Mom." There, he had said it. It all felt like one big nightmare. But he knew it was real and it wasn't going to go away.

"I know, David. I am here for you and will do anything in this world you need me to do to help. But for now, I know you need to be here with your dad. We can talk about your mom's arrangements when you are ready.

"Oh man, David." Rick suddenly thought about the safe in John's office.

"What, Rick?"

"You know how your dad is. He plans for everything. He has a safe in his office, and there are papers in there. John told me if anything ever happened, to be sure to tell you about it and to give you the key."

"What's in it, Rick?"

"I'm not sure what all he has in there, but I know he and Nikki did a will and prepared all the legal papers necessary to make sure that you and your brothers knew their wishes in case anything ever happened. You know your dad…always having all his bases covered."

David looked down at the clothes he was wearing from the night before. He had already gone to bed when Rick had called, and had thrown on an old pair of jeans and a t-shirt to come to the hospital. He needed a shower and a change of clothes, but he wasn't about to go anywhere until he knew his dad was going to be ok.

"I am going to take a walk and get some fresh air. I need to call Linda. She will be wondering what's going on."

"Will you please tell her to call Jessica? I know she's worried sick. Tell her that I will call her just as soon as I can."

"Any word on Dad?" Chris was carrying a couple of cups of coffee and Charlie had a plate with some donuts and a couple of blueberry muffins.

"Not yet." David wasn't hungry, but reached for one of the cups. He hoped the caffeine would help his headache.

"When can we see Dad?" Charlie asked. David could tell he had been crying again.

He walked over to Charlie and hugged him. He didn't know what to say to his little brother to make it all better.

"Good morning." They looked up to see Dr. Lewis standing in the doorway.

"Good morning, Dr. Lewis. How's Dad? Has he regained consciousness? Can we go see him now?" Chris walked toward him.

"No, I am sorry, he is still unconscious. I'm glad you are all here. Your dad made it through the night, but I am afraid there is no improvement in his condition. He doesn't seem to be responding well to the medications, and we can't keep his blood pressure up. There is some cranial swelling, and I am concerned about the pressure on his brain. Infection is another concern. His temperature has been climbing through the night. We are going to change medications and see how he responds. I know you want to see your father, but let's try to get him stabilized first."

"Dr. Lewis, please tell Dad we are here," Chris said.

"And tell him that we love him," Charlie added.

"Yes, I will. Please know that we are doing everything humanly possible for your father," Dr. Lewis assured them. "A lot will depend on your father, and he is a fighter. I see he has a lot to fight for. I don't know how you feel about the power of prayer, but I have found that it never hurts to ask for some help from the Man Upstairs." Dr. Lewis turned and headed back toward ICU.

Chris managed a smile. "One of my first memories as a little boy is of Dad teaching me to pray every night before I went to sleep. He would like the fact that his doctor is a 'man of faith'. You know, Dad says there aren't enough of them around anymore. Right, David? David?"

David was gone. He was already headed to the Chapel.

Dad, is that you?
YES, SON, IT'S DAD.
Dad, is it really you?
YES, SON, IT IS REALLY ME.
Oh Dad, I have missed you so much.
I KNOW, SON, I HAVE MISSED YOU, TOO.
You left when I was so young, Dad. I wasn't ready to say goodbye.
I KNOW, JOHN, I AM SORRY.
It wasn't your fault. It was just hard, you know… especially for Mom. She never was the same after you left us. She tried her best, for me, you know, but the day you died, the best part of Mom died with you. She got so sick.
YOUR MOM AND I ARE SO PROUD OF YOU, SON.
You've seen her? Mom is alright?
YES, SHE IS FINE.
I wish you and Mom could see my boys. I have been blessed with three awesome boys.

23

OH, SON, I KNOW. THEY ARE FINE BOYS, AND YOUR MOM AND I ARE SO VERY PROUD OF THEM AND OF YOU.

You taught me so much, Dad. In the fifteen short years I had you with me, you taught me a lifetime of lessons to take with me. I have tried to pass those same lessons on to my boys. Thank you for being such a good father. I never got the chance to tell you how much you meant to me.

YOU THANKED ME A MILLION TIMES, JOHN...BY BEING AN EVEN BETTER FATHER TO YOUR BOYS THAN I WAS TO YOU. I AM SO PROUD OF YOU, SON.

I am glad you are here, Dad. Things are in a real mess, and I don't know what to do. You always knew what was best. The boys have lost their mother, they need me, and I am not able to be there for them. It is tearing me up to see them going through this. They need me now more than ever. But I am hurt bad, Dad, and I am tired. I have tried, but I don't have the strength to fight anymore. It feels so good to be with you again. I have missed you. I want to go with you to see Mom. Mom will hold me and make everything alright. We can all be together again. Will you please take me to her, Dad? Please? I have missed her so much! I am so tired. I am going to sleep for awhile now, Dad. Don't leave me again. Stay here with me while I sleep...just like you used to. When I wake up, we can go see Mom.

OKAY, SON, YOU GET SOME REST NOW.

"David, they want to see us all in the family room right away." Chris had found him still in the Chapel.

David got up and walked slowly behind Chris. When they got to the family room, Rick was there, and Linda was there, too. She was sitting on the couch with Charlie. David looked around at everyone. No one was making eye contact. He knew the news would not be good, and he was trying to prepare himself for whatever was going to hit next.

The silence in the room was deafening. Rick finally spoke without ever looking up. "They requested that the family be called in. I called Jessica, David. I knew she would want to be here with you. She was going to get your neighbor to keep Allison and she was going to be here as soon as she could get here."

David nodded. His head still hurt and now his stomach was hurting, too. How could everything have gone so wrong? This was supposed to be a special day. They were supposed to be at home getting ready for a cookout to celebrate their Moms' fiftieth birthday. Instead, they were all gathered in a room in a hospital waiting to see if they would be burying their dad along with their mom. How do you deal with something like that? He looked over at Charlie. He had to hold it together. He closed his eyes and took a deep breath.

David opened his eyes and saw Jessica standing in the doorway. He rushed to her and grabbed her and held her. He felt her arms wrapped tightly around him and leaned over and softly whispered in her ear. "I love you, Jess. I am glad you are here, Sweetheart." Then he quietly thanked God for sending him a lifeline.

"Oh David, I love you, too." David could feel some strength slowly return to his body. He and Jessica walked over to the couch and sat down next to Charlie.

They recognized the voice from the night before in their dad's room. "Were you able to get any sleep last night?" the nurse asked. She continued on without waiting for a response. "Dr. Lewis called in Dr. Liebovich for Mr. Hughes before he left the hospital this morning. Dr. Liebovich is highly trained in brain trauma cases such as your father's. He will be in shortly to talk to all of you."

Chris studied her face as she talked. He looked at her name pinned to her nurse's uniform. Clara Fulton. Her face was sweet. Her voice was calm and reassuring. But he could see the concern in her eyes. He knew that for every word she was saying, there were a lot more that she wasn't. He knew Dr. Liebovich wouldn't have anything to say that he wanted to hear. He had never felt such dread and fear. There was no way he could joke his way out of this one. He felt sick. He sat down in the chair he had tried to sleep in the night before.

There was that silence again. They all sat in silence for what seemed like hours. Finally Dr. Liebovich stood there with them in the room. He was tall and thin and looked to be in his early sixties. His hair was long and his glasses noticeably thick. He took them off and looked at each one of them, taking his time to somehow connect to them without ever speaking a word.

He finally spoke. "I am sorry. Mr. Hughes is not responding to our treatment. We had hoped to reverse his condition, but that has not happened. We are now dealing with brain herniation, and I am afraid you need to prepare yourself…I don't expect him to live through the day."

David swallowed hard. "Herniation?" His voice cracked.

"Yes, we have not been able to control the swelling of his brain. When you hit your thumb with a hammer, it swells. The same thing happens when the brain gets hit, but the problem is the skull restricts the space the brain has to swell. The swelling causes the internal pressure of the brain to rise. The breathing and the heartbeat are then affected and the brain will begin to hemorrhage. We are already seeing some signs of bleeding. I am so sorry."

No one moved a muscle as Dr. Liebovich exited the room. It was as if time stood still…as if by freezing this moment, they wouldn't have to take in anything else to have to deal with.

Chris finally stood up. "NO! I won't sit here and do nothing. Where there is life, there is hope. Isn't that what Dad always said? No matter what, he never gave up on me and now we won't give up on Dad!"

David and Charlie stood and followed their brother back to the hospital Chapel to pray for a miracle.

"Mr. Hughes, I need for you to listen to me. My name is Clara and I have been taking care of you since you were brought in last night. I know you are tired and I know you don't have much strength left. But we have done all we can for you. It's all up to you now. You have to fight with everything you have. You have to do it for those three fine boys of yours. I just went to check on them during my lunch break and found them all in the Chapel praying to God to bring you back to them. They need you, Mr. Hughes. You have to fight. It's all up to you now."

Mom and Dad

I had great parents.

My dad was John David Hughes, Sr., affectionately known to everyone as J. D. He was a big, jolly man who loved life and loved people and loved to laugh. He loved a good story, and would always make sure there was a lesson to be learned in any he told.

"Everyone matters, John," he would say. "No matter what one's background or circumstance in life, they are important, and you treat them with kindness and respect.

"When you meet someone, you greet them with a smile. You show them you are glad to see them. You give them a firm handshake and you look them in the eyes. You can't trust someone who won't look you in the eyes.

"And always remember the Golden Rule, Son. You treat others like you would want to be treated."

Dad was a good man and everyone respected and trusted him.

I loved to hear him talk of what he called the 'olden days'...the days of his youth.

He was born and raised in a small farm community about thirty miles west of Chicago. Times were tough for the small family-owned farms, and many of the kids he grew up with had to stay out of school a lot to help out at home, especially when the crops were coming in. But Dad said his father never allowed him to miss a day of school. He was raised to work hard, but that nothing got in the way of his education.

So, his father would have him up before sunrise getting his chores done. He would then head on foot to the little school house down the dirt road about a mile away. He worked in the fields after school until the sun went down, and then studied late into the night.

After he graduated from high school, he went to Chicago to attend college. He got a job working in a drug store near the campus, and made the decision to one day own his own drug store back home. He became a pharmacist and saved every dollar he could out of each paycheck. When he was thirty-two years old, he left Chicago and returned home and bought his own little store.

Dad loved what he did. Besides the pharmacy, he sold gifts such as jewelry and perfumes and he had records and magazines and books. He had a little snack shop and soda fountain in one corner of the store. The kids would come in after school and buy chips and cherry cokes and ice cream floats and catch up on all the gossip of the day. The local men would come in on Saturday mornings and drink coffee and discuss the weather and their crops and politics and in general, solve all the problems of the world.

"Everyone has an opinion, John," Dad would say. "And when you hear two sides to a story, you can be assured that the truth lies somewhere in the middle." Dad was fascinated with human nature and what made people tick, and he loved that his drug store kept him in contact with everyone in the community.

When he would talk about those days, he would say that between his schooling and working, he hadn't had the time for girls. However, I always doubted that to be totally true. I suspected he had made some time for a 'lady friend' on occasion. But, for sure, no one special had come along as yet…that is, not until a 'pretty little Southern gal' happened into the store one afternoon.

My mom, Mary Elizabeth Clark, was born and raised in Georgia. She was from a family of twelve, and also knew what hard work was all about. She was from a time and place where most married young and lived and raised their family close to where they had grown up.

Mom's baby brother, Uncle Sid, always said my mom 'marched to the beat of a different drummer'. "She was a dreamer, John," he would say. "She would love to go to town and look at those Hollywood magazines and read all about the movie stars and see what they were wearing and who was marrying who." Uncle Sid would laugh and continue, "She had a whole slew of potential suitors coming 'round, and she had no interest in none of them. She would have Daddy run them off. Said those boys were silly.

"When your mama got old enough that they couldn't stop her, she got up enough money for a bus ticket to Chicago. We had a cousin who lived out from the city, and she said Mary Elizabeth could come live with her. Mama cried and Daddy said not to worry, she would be back. Besides, it's not really Chicago, Mama. It's a little place just like here. The girl will be fine.

"Mary Elizabeth said there was a great big world out there, and she was going to experience all of it she could. And Daddy was mistaken; your mama never came back...well, not except for a visit every now and then."

Mom loved to tell me about the first time she ever saw Dad. She had been in town for about a week and had been trying to find work. She was tired and thirsty and went inside a small little drug store to sit and rest her feet and have a coke.

The place was busy, and she picked up a magazine to look through while she waited. Jacqueline Kennedy was on the cover, and she studied her dress and hat and gloves and purse and dreamed of the day when she could have an outfit like that. She looked down at the blue cotton dress her mama had made her before she left home. "Mama could make something like that if she set her mind to it," she thought. She wondered what Mama was cooking for supper and what kind of trouble the boys had gotten into that day.

"Can I help you, Little Lady?" Mom said she looked up to see the kindest eyes she had ever seen in her life. "They just lit up when he looked at me, John."

"Why yes, I would love a fountain coke, thank you," she had answered.

"A Southern Gal...I love that accent. Where are you from?" he had asked.

"I'm from Georgia, Sir, and I am no Gal." Mom said that was the first time she heard my dad laugh, and she knew at that very moment she wanted to hear that laugh for the rest of her life.

"Point well taken, Ma'am. And what shall I call you then?"

"My name is Mary Elizabeth."

"Then Mary Elizabeth it is." Dad had handed Mom her fountain drink that day and couldn't take his eyes off her as he tried to wait on all the customers. "He made me blush when he kept looking at me that way."

Dad would then chime in on the story at this point and say, "How could I not keep on looking? I had just seen the prettiest Little Lady I ever did see."

"How much do I owe you?" she had asked as she got up to leave.

"This one is on the house."

"You can't make any money by giving your drinks away. And you look like you could use some help around here."

"I never thought about it, but yes, I could definitely use some help."

"I just happen to need a job."

"Then you just happen to be hired."

"And from that day on, your dad and I never spent a day apart," Mom would tell me. It was a great story and I loved to see how happy it made her to tell it.

They made a great team. Mom loved working the snack shop and selling the gifts and perfumes. Dad ran the pharmacy, and the business thrived. When the store closed each day, they would go out to dinner and take long walks or go to the movies. They talked of their pasts and their hopes and dreams for their futures, and it was obvious to everyone who knew them that there would be a wedding real soon.

On Sundays after church, they would drive into the city and take in the sites, and on a beautiful fall afternoon in a Chicago park, John David Hughes asked Mary Elizabeth Clark to be his wife. She graciously accepted. They were married on Christmas day exactly six months after their first meeting that day in the drug store.

Mom called me her little miracle. She desperately wanted to have a baby, and after two miscarriages, her doctors told her she would not be able to have any children. "I decided to prove them all wrong," she would say. And that is just what she did.

After I was born, Mom stayed at home with me until I got old enough to go to school. She would help at the store until school was out, then pick me up and have a big meal fixed by the time Dad got home.

Mom loved music. She loved Elvis and the Beatles and the Beach Boys. She would put an album on the record player while she and Dad washed the dishes. Dad would grab her up when a song he especially liked would start playing, and dance with her right there in the kitchen. Mom would motion for me to join them, and the three of us would dance and laugh and sing to the music. I loved our times together.

Mom would take me to the Saturday afternoon matinees. She loved the movies and especially enjoyed watching Elvis and John Wayne and the James Bond films. "If I hadn't met your dad, I guess I would have just had to marry Elvis Presley, John." She loved to try to get a reaction out of me. "What do you think about that?"

"Well, I think it would be bad if you were already married to Elvis when you finally met Dad." I tried to imagine Elvis being my dad. "I'm glad you married Dad."

Mom would laugh and grab my hand and skip down the street. "I am glad, too, Baby Boy."

My favorite day was Sunday. The drug store was closed. Dad would get up early and fix a breakfast of bacon and pancakes and grits. Mom said you couldn't have a decent breakfast without grits, and Dad learned to love them. After breakfast, we would dress and go to church. We would take long drives, and on nice days, go to the park for a picnic. Dad and I would throw the football and Mom would jump up and down and cheer us on.

When I got old enough, Dad let me come to the store and work with him. I would work a couple of hours after school, then a few days a week during the summer. He wanted me to have some fun, too. "You will have to work your whole life, Son," he would say. "Go have some fun." So I would go to the Lake swimming with my buddies or to the bowling alley to bowl or to shoot some pool. But my favorite times were at the store with my mom and dad. Life was good and we were happy.

It was the summer of my fifteenth year. "John, come eat breakfast." Mom stuck her head in my bedroom door again. "John, get up…your eggs are getting cold."

Dad was already at the table, all dressed and in a great mood as always. "Good morning, John. How did you sleep?"

"Good," I had mumbled.

"Wake up, Sleepy Head," he laughed. "Are you coming into work today?"

"I thought I would go swimming this morning, if it's alright."

"That sounds like a plan. The water will feel good in this heat. It is supposed to reach the high 90's today."

Dad finished his breakfast and told Mom how good it was. He told her she looked beautiful and kissed her just as he always did. He told me to have a good day and affectionately tousled my hair as he walked by. "Someone needs a haircut." He winked at me.

"You have a good day, too, Dad. I will be in to work later this afternoon."

He was almost out the door and turned around and came back to Mom. "I love you, Pretty Lady," he said as he kissed her again.

"I love you, too, J. D."

Dad waved as he walked out the door and it closed behind him.

"See, John, your dad's eyes still light up to this day when he looks at me. I hope you meet someone someday who makes your eyes light up like that."

"Oh, Mom."

She laughed. That was the last time I ever heard her laugh like that.

Dad had been gone about thirty minutes. The doorbell rang. Mr. Williams, who owned the hardware store next door to the drug store, was standing there. "J. D. has been taken to the hospital. He fell out in front of the store while unlocking the door. I think it's his heart, Mary Elizabeth."

Dad was gone before the ambulance got him to the hospital. They said he had a massive heart attack. I guess I went into shock, because everything about that time is pretty much a blur to me. I just remember they had to sedate Mom and there were so many people at the funeral until they didn't have enough room for everyone to sit inside the church. Everyone in our community came by to see how we were doing. They sent flowers and brought food and sent cards.

Mom seemed to grow thinner and weaker in the coming weeks. Everyone noticed, and was worried about her, but thought it was normal for her to be depressed and to be in such grief with the sudden death of someone she had been so close to for all those years.

Some of the family came to stay with us to help out. I guess I was still in shock, because I don't remember much about those days, either. I don't remember who all came and went and who did what. I just remember Mom couldn't eat or sleep. And I remember that everyone got more and more worried about her.

By the time they found the cancer, it had pretty much taken over her frail, thin body. She tried her best to fight. But as the weeks passed, she was in more and more pain, and I knew she was losing her battle. The doctors told the family they couldn't do anymore for her than try to keep her as comfortable as possible. She refused to spend her last days in a hospital and insisted she wanted to be at home.

I marked another day off the calendar in my room. Nine months had passed since Dad had died. I heard Mom moaning in her bedroom next to mine. The pain had been unbearable that day. They said it was the cancer taking her life away, but I wondered if her broken heart was killing her even faster than the cancer. I knew she missed Dad terribly. I knew she was worried about me. She was hurting and trying to keep her moans quiet so I wouldn't hear. My heart hurt.

I went into her room. "You need anything, Mom?"

"Hi, my sweet boy. I just need you to lie down beside me." Her voice was so weak.

"I love you, Mom."

She wrapped her arms around me and ran her fingers through my hair and wiped the tears that ran down my face. "I've had a good life, Baby Boy. Don't be sad for me."

I lay there listening to her fight for each breath.

"You've been through so much.   I don't want to leave you." Her voice was barely a whisper.

"It's okay, Mom. I am going to be alright."

"I know you are, John. You are a strong man. And a good man, too. Just like your dad. I love you so much."

That's the first time Mom had ever referred to me as a man rather than her baby boy. It was as if she needed to see me as a man that night and to hear me say I was going to be alright so she could give herself permission to give up the fight. Mom passed away a few hours later in her sleep. And that night, at the age of sixteen, I truly did have to become a man.

Dad, are you still here?

YES, SON, I AM STILL HERE.

I had a dream about us...about when we were all together. I'm ready to go now, Dad. Let's go see Mom.

"Code Red. Get Dr. Liebovich in here STAT. We're losing him."

YOU HAVE TO GO BACK, SON. YOU CAN'T GO WITH ME. THE NURSE WAS RIGHT, YOU KNOW. YOUR BOYS NEED YOU.

I can't, Dad.

JOHN, YOU CAN DO IT. YOU GO BACK AND FIGHT LIKE YOU'VE NEVER FOUGHT BEFORE. WE WILL ALL BE TOGETHER AGAIN SOMEDAY. BUT IT'S NOT TIME YET.

Dad, are you sure?

YOU GO BACK TO THEM, SON. GO BACK NOW BEFORE IT'S TOO LATE.

Dad?

IT'S THE RIGHT THING TO DO.

Yes, the right thing...Got to go back...Can do it

Bye Dad...

David...Chris...Charlie...my boys...

Can do it...

It's a Miracle

David opened his eyes. He had fallen asleep. Charlie was still sitting between him and Chris on the front bench in the Chapel. He looked at his watch. It was mid-afternoon. "Why have we not heard any more from the doctors?" he wondered aloud.

Chris shook his head. "Right now I am hoping no news is good news."

David's stomach still hurt. He hadn't eaten all day, and the coffee he drank earlier on an empty stomach hadn't helped at all. He could feel the acid slowly rising in his throat. "You have my stomach, Son," Dad would say. "All of our emotions go straight to our stomach." He knew he needed to eat, but he couldn't.

He was worried about Charlie and Chris. He was the big brother and he was supposed to know what to do to help them. But he felt helpless. Everything was out of his control. There was a throbbing pain in his head now.

He put his hand on Charlie's shoulder. Charlie jumped. "Hey, Charlie, let's go check on Rick and the girls. I need to find some aspirin." David motioned for Chris to come with them.

"You go on. I'm going to stay here for a little while longer." That was the first time Charlie had spoken all afternoon.

Chris and David walked to the door. "Should I stay with him?"

David looked around. Charlie had gotten off the bench and was on his knees at the altar. "Let's give him some time alone."

They walked back to the family room. David walked over to Rick. "Any word?"

"No, nothing. It's been too long. Why have they not come to tell us what's going on in there?"

"I know. Man, this waiting…I want to hear something, but then again, I don't want to hear."

"I know what you mean."

David went over to the chair where Jessica was sitting. "Do you have any aspirin? My head is killing me."

She reached in her purse and pulled out a bottle of aspirin and gave him a couple. "There is a coke machine down the hall. Who all wants a coke?" She got out of the chair. Rick got a couple of dollars out of his wallet and handed them to her. "Whatever you get will be fine."

"I'll go with you." David walked down the hall with Jessica. When they got to the coke machine, he put some money in the change slot and got a Mountain Dew. He put the two aspirin in his mouth and took a big gulp. He felt sick. There was a restroom across the hall, and he ran through the door to the toilet. He leaned over it just in time and threw up the aspirin and the Mountain Dew and the acid that was in his stomach.

The restroom had a sign on the door that said 'Men', but Jessica went in behind him. She tore off some paper towels and ran cold water on them and put them on David's forehead.

"Mom is dead, Baby. And I feel like I am waiting for them to come tell me Dad is dead, too." David started crying and he couldn't stop.

"Get it out, Honey. It's okay, get it out." She held him and cried with him.

"Dad is going to be alright."

David and Jessica looked over to see Charlie standing inside the restroom door.

"Don't cry, you guys. He's really going to be alright."

David went over to Charlie. "Did you hear from the doctors, Charlie?"

"No."

David looked over at Jessica.

Charlie continued. "I was in the Chapel and I was praying like I've never prayed before. And I felt this arm around me and I turned around to see who it was, and there was no one there. And then I heard this voice. And he told me not to be afraid, that my dad was going to be alright."

David didn't know what to say. He didn't want Charlie to think he didn't believe him, but he also didn't want him to get his hopes up in case the news was bad. And Dr. Liebovich had told them the news would more than likely be bad.

David chose his words carefully. "Charlie, you've been under a lot of stress, and you've had no rest. Do you think maybe you dozed off and had a dream?"

"No, David, it really happened. I was wide awake, and the voice was as real as yours is right now. I know it happened."

"Who do you think spoke to you, Charlie?"

"It was my guardian angel, David. You know Dad has always told us we have a guardian angel looking out for us. God sent him to me so I wouldn't have to worry anymore. Dad is going to be alright. You'll see."

They walked back to the family room and joined the others. They didn't have any drinks with them, and no one seemed to notice. No one talked about what happened in the restroom. They all continued to sit and wait.

Twenty minutes had passed since Dr. Liebovich had gotten the page to come STAT to ICU. His patient's heart had stopped beating and the heart monitor had already flat-lined. His attempts to resuscitate Mr. Hughes had failed. Dr. Liebovich picked up the chart and looked at his watch to record the time of death.

Dr. Lewis had told Dr. Liebovich that Mr. Hughes' wife had been killed in the same accident. He thought about the family waiting for word on their loved one. He had so hoped this guy would make it. He looked over the chart and reviewed all the medical procedures performed since they had brought him in. He felt assured that everything medically possible had been done for him.

He had instructed the nurses to clear the equipment. They had unhooked the ventilator, and as they were about to unhook the heart monitor, it had slowly started to beep with life. Mr. Hughes had mysteriously started to breathe on his own.

"Well, I'll be…" Dr. Liebovich continued to stare at the monitors in amazement as the blood pressure and cranial pressure readings slowly began to return to normal. The heartbeat was strong now. "There is certainly no medical explanation for this," he said.

"I am going to go call Dr. Lewis. I have to tell him what just happened here." Dr. Liebovich made a notation on the chart. "Nurse Fulton, call me immediately if there are any changes. I will be back in a few minutes. If everything still looks this good when I get back, we will have some very encouraging news for his family."

Nurse Clara Fulton watched Dr. Liebovich walk down the hall. She got a tissue and wiped the tears streaming down her cheeks. Days like this made it all worthwhile. "Welcome back, Mr. Hughes," she said.

She looked at the chart. She noticed three words scribbled in the space where Dr. Liebovich was going to record the time of death moments earlier. She read the words aloud. "IT'S A MIRACLE!"

Dr. Liebovich was standing there with them again. "I am sorry you've had to wait so long to hear from me." He took his glasses off as he had done before.

David looked over at Charlie. Charlie looked at peace and didn't have the worry on his face that the rest of them had.

Chris took a deep breath. He looked Dr. Liebovich squarely in the eyes. Something was different about his demeanor this time. His expression wasn't so solemn.

"I told you earlier that we didn't expect Mr. Hughes to live through the day. To be honest with you, I didn't expect him to live through the hour. And we did have a very close call. I have never heard of anyone living after their cranial pressure readings climbed that high.

"However, it seems your father has decided to defy medical odds today and prove us wrong. He seems to be responding well to the medication now and his condition has been stabilized for the past hour." Dr. Liebovich continued, a hint of caution in his voice. "We are going to gradually start weaning him off some of the medications, slowly wake him up, and see how he responds."

Chris breathed a sigh of relief. "Then will Dad be out of his coma?"

"We have no way of knowing. There was extensive edema, or swelling of the brain. We don't know how much damage there is, but the brain has a remarkable ability to heal, and I have never seen anyone with the will to live that your father has. Let's proceed with cautious optimism and see what happens.

"Now, how would you like to go with me to see your father?"

A Time to Live and Die

'To everything there is a season, and a time to every purpose under the heaven...'

David listened as the pastor talked about God having a plan for each of us. He said we don't always understand the things that happen in our lives, but God is in control, and one day all things will be revealed. David found comfort in the fact that all things happen for a reason, and one day all this chaos would make sense.

Today was particularly bittersweet. A week had passed since the accident and here they were at their mom's memorial service. Their dad was being moved to a private room and David's thoughts went back to the hospital. He knew there were many unresolved issues and emotions with his mom, but he would deal with them later.

'A time to be born, and a time to die.' He thought of Solomon's words recorded centuries ago, and marveled at how much they applied to his life right now, in this very moment in time. He thought of Allison. Jessica sat next to him. He sat with his arm around her and gently squeezed her shoulder. How blessed he was to have such a good wife and such a good mom for his little girl.

Charlie sat between him and Chris, and Paige sat next to Chris. He could feel the pew shake as Charlie quietly sobbed. Charlie was having a tough time. David was glad Charlie had been able to have a good relationship with his mom for as much of his life as he could remember. He and Chris could not say the same. Their mother had not been emotionally available to them for most of their early years. David was thankful things had gotten better at home after Charlie was born. He was thankful for some good memories of his mom. His thoughts went back to the hospital and he began to wonder how his dad was doing.

Six days earlier, Dr. Liebovich had led them to their father's room. Dr. Lewis had come in soon behind them and had been pleased with everything he saw. "This is indeed miraculous," he had said.

Dr. Lewis had reiterated what Dr. Liebovich had said and had cautioned them their Dad was still very critical. They couldn't be sure of what damage there had been to his brain, and they couldn't be sure if he would come out of the coma, or what condition he would be in if he did.

He had remained in stable condition. Once the doctors were confident enough time had passed that there was no concern of infection setting in, they said he could be moved to a private room. It would be nice to be able to stay with him instead of being limited to the short visits in ICU three times a day.

David knew his dad would be upset that he wasn't able to be with them at the memorial service. That is, if he ever woke up. Charlie had corrected him anytime he had used the word 'if' and said, "You mean WHEN Dad wakes up." And at this point, he tended to believe him. He now believed what happened to Charlie that day in the Chapel was real. How ironic it had been that he had learned more about faith this week from his little brother than he had learned his entire life. "What's the point in praying if you don't have the faith to believe it can come true?" Charlie had asked.

"There is no way this attorney can argue that point," he had answered him.

After we all had visited with Dad for awhile that day, Dr. Lewis had met with Chris, Charlie and me back in the family room and had a long talk with us. He explained this waiting could go on for quite awhile. He told us it was important we get some rest and eat something and take turns being at the hospital while we waited on Dad's condition to improve. He had convinced us the best thing we could do for our father was to take good care of ourselves so we could hold out, that we would be no good to him or anyone else if we got sick or run down.

Linda sat us down after he left. We were all exhausted and not thinking straight, so it was good to have someone take charge. She explained she had gotten some sleep the night before, and she would stay there at the hospital. She said we should all go home and eat and get a shower and get some sleep. She assured us that if there was any change whatsoever, she would call immediately.

Jessica told Charlie and Chris and Rick to come over to our house and she would fix everyone something to eat. They could shower and sleep for awhile and get rested before they came back to the hospital.

David had wanted to go straight home to see Allison, but had remembered the safe Rick had told him about. "Rick, let's go by the office first."

Rick had taken a key out of his desk drawer and had opened the safe for David. David had found some insurance papers, some CD's and stock and bond certificates, and a folder labeled 'Last Will and Testament'. Also, there were some letters and correspondences his Dad had saved. One letter was especially old, and he noticed it was written to his dad from his Grandfather Hughes. David made a mental note that one day he would ask him if it would be alright to read it.

He finally found what he was looking for…a folder marked 'in case of death'. David pulled it out and sat at his dad's desk and began to look through it. Just as Rick had said, his dad and mom had made all the necessary arrangements in case something happened to them. The funeral home was listed and all arrangements were not only made in advance, but paid for.

"Can you believe Dad did all this at such a young age? These papers were drawn up over ten years ago."

David looked over at Rick. He was slumped over his desk sound asleep. David knew they needed to get home and get some rest, so he grabbed the folder and started to put all the papers back inside the safe. There was one more envelope pushed to the back he had not seen.

He pulled it out. On the outside was an address in South Carolina. He looked inside the envelope and there was a picture of a young woman. She looked to be in her mid to late twenties with long, brown, thick hair. She was quite beautiful and David noticed her striking green eyes. He wondered how old the picture was. He looked on the back and written in pencil was the name, 'Brooke'.

"Who is Brooke?"

Rick immediately woke up and straightened up in his chair. "Brooke?"

"Yes, I don't remember Dad ever mentioning anyone by that name. I don't recall anyone in our family named Brooke."

Rick was noticeably uncomfortable. "That's something you'll have to ask John about."

David was too tired to pursue who this mystery woman was. He put the envelope back with all the other papers and locked the safe back up.

He put the file with the funeral arrangements under his arm. "Let's go home," he said to Rick, handing him the key. "You okay?"

"I'll be fine once I get some rest."

"Yea, Rick, thanks for everything." David hugged Rick. "I don't know what we would have done without your help and support through all this."

They had eaten the hamburgers and fries Jessica had fixed. They had showered and slept and had taken turns at the hospital through the rest of the week.

Linda was singing 'The Lord's Prayer'. She had an amazing voice. His mom had requested it sung in the arrangements she and Dad had made. She would have been pleased with the beautiful version Linda had chosen.

David was fighting back the tears now.

'For thine is the kingdom, and the power, and the glory...forever... Amen.'

The service was ending.

At that moment, David was able to make peace with his feelings and feel complete forgiveness in his heart. He quietly whispered the words as Linda concluded 'The Lord's Prayer'.

"Bye, Mom. I love you."

Life's Lessons

Eric Clapton played on the little stereo David had brought from home. The doctors had told them it was important to keep their dad's brain stimulated...to talk to him, to play music, and to exercise his feet and arms several times a day.

"You never know what will trigger a response," Nurse Fulton was saying as she rubbed his arms. She and an orderly had been in to give him a bath and change his hospital gown and the sheets on his bed. David had been right there helping them with whatever they needed him to do.

"You have a fine one here, Mr. Hughes," Nurse Fulton had said. "Good looking, too. If only I were a little younger," she laughed.

"Now, who says you are too old for me?" David laughed with her.

"Oh, and I see he's a charmer, too. I bet he gets that honest, Mr. Hughes. Something tells me you are quite the charmer yourself."

I can't wait until the day I can thank you for taking such good care of me, Miss Clara. You are such a sweetheart. You have been so good to my boys. I might just have to send you some roses, sweet lady. Yes, send roses...that is exactly what I will do.

"So, Mr. Hughes likes Eric Clapton?" She recognized the 'Pilgrim' cd playing on the stereo. "I am quite a blues fan myself, you know."

"Yea, he's one of Dad's favorites. Dad likes all kinds of music."

Nurse Fulton took his temperature and blood pressure and checked the IV bags. "Everything looks good; you call us if you need anything."

David sat back down in the recliner by his father's bed. His new job wasn't scheduled to start until the end of the month. The partners at the new firm he was joining had been by to check on how things were going and to give their condolences. They had assured him he could have as much time as he needed before starting to work.

It hadn't been easy, but David and Chris had finally convinced Charlie to go back to school. He didn't need to get any further behind in his classes, and they knew it would be good for him to get back to a somewhat normal routine. "Dad would want you back in school, Charlie," they had told him. He was staying with Rick and Linda, and they were bringing him to the hospital every afternoon after school for a visit.

Chris was trying to work some, but he was having a hard time concentrating, and wanted to be at the hospital as much as possible. Besides, he knew David needed a break every other night or so. "We are in this together, Big Brother," he had said.

'My Father's Eyes' played on the stereo. His dad loved that song. "I have the best Dad anyone could have." David said these words aloud to his father.

David got up and moved to the bed. He massaged his dad's arms and legs and moved them up and down very slowly as the nurses had instructed him to do. "They said it's important to keep you moving and limber, Dad."

It was so hard to see him like this. The 'what ifs' were starting. The questions that had been haunting him were finally starting to form in his head. "What if he never wakes up? What if he has to spend the rest of his life in a vegetative state?" The thoughts were more than David could bear. He knew his dad wouldn't want to live like that. "What if their prayers had been selfish?" They had prayed to have their father with them, no matter what. But at what cost? He went outside and paced the halls. "You have to get a grip, David," he said to himself.

He walked back into the room and took his dad's hand. "Dad, do you remember the fishing trip we took that summer, just you and me?"

Sure I do, Son.

David squeezed his dad's hand and smiled as he began to recall the details of their trip. He leaned closer to his father as he began to speak. "I remember we caught a lot of fish on that trip, but that wasn't the best part of it for me. What I remember most about that trip are the great talks we had out in that boat. Some of the most valuable lessons you ever taught me were on that trip. If worms had machine guns…you remember telling me that story, Dad?"

Oh yea, David, I remember it well. Your Grandfather Hughes taught me many valuable lessons in life, but none so valuable as the ones I learned as a twelve year old boy. That day in the boat, I wanted to pass those same lessons on to you, Son. If worms had machine guns…my dad's favorite story to tell.

Yes, I was twelve years old. There had been a crime of rape committed in a neighboring county, and the trial had been moved to our little community. The courthouse was only a block away from the drug store.

The drug store had become the gathering place for many, to meet and discuss the proceedings of the day, and to give their opinion as to what the verdict should be. It was becoming obvious to everyone who heard the facts of the case that the man on trial was guilty. The interest seemed to grow with each passing day.

Mom and Dad had tried to protect me from the particulars of the case, but as emotions had become more heated and the trial was talked about more and more, they were faced with a flood of questions from a curious twelve-year old. They finally had to sit me down and explain the concept of rape as delicately as they possibly could.

"How can anyone do something so bad?" I had asked.

"That's a very good question, Son," my dad had answered me that day. "People are capable of doing some very good things, but they are also capable of doing some very bad things, too."

The trial was finally winding down and the attorneys had given their closing statements. "It's all up to the jury now. No way will they find him anything but guilty," someone had said that day in the store. And everyone seemed to agree.

Mom had stayed home with me after school those last days of the trial. She and Dad agreed that they didn't want me at the store with all the gruesome details of the case being discussed. That night as Dad sat down at the dinner table, he told Mom the case had gone to the jury. "So we should be hearing something real soon," he said.

"I'm just ready for them to find him guilty and this whole thing be done with, J. D.," Mom had commented.

"You know, Mary Elizabeth, everyone thinks he will be found guilty but ole Chester. He said it is a crying shame what was done to that girl. And he said there is not a doubt in his mind that the boy standing trial is guilty as sin. But Chester found out the boy comes from a mighty wealthy and influential family in the city. He said he's been watching those defense attorneys real close, and they are sitting there way too smug and confident. Chester believes they are somehow going to be able to get that boy acquitted."

"Surely not, J. D." Mom was saddened at the thought of someone committing such an act and going free.

"What is *acquitted?*" I asked.

"That means they find him not guilty," Dad answered. He assured me our justice system was a good one but said, like everything else, it wasn't perfect. He explained that when someone has a lot of money, they can sometimes pay for things to go their way. "Money talks, Son," Dad had told me that day. "There is nothing wrong with having money, but it's sure wrong to misuse it. And it's wrong when having a lot of money makes you think you are above the law or better than another person. And we have to remember, John, we weren't there. We can't be too quick to judge. Under our law, a person is innocent until proven guilty."

Mom and I were anxious for Dad to get home the next evening. He walked in the door shaking his head.

"No, J. D., they surely didn't let that boy go."

"I'm afraid so, Mary Elizabeth. Ole Chester was right. Most everyone thinks they were somehow able to get to the jurors and 'convince them' to vote their way.

"You know, I was thinking today how 'funny' life is. I mean, everyone has become so involved in it all. But soon life will go on just as before, and for the most part, it will all be forgotten. That is, except for that poor girl who will have to live with it from now on. I can't imagine how it feels to have to sit there and tell complete strangers the awful things that someone did to you and have to sit there and face him in a courtroom. Then for a jury to come back and say we don't believe you, we say let him go. I tell you, if that happened to my sister…"

Dad went to wash his hands and sat down at the dining table. "Anyway, you won't believe what happened in the store this afternoon. I tell you, in all my years, I have never seen anything like it before."

"What happened, J. D.?"

"Yea, what happened, Dad?"

"I was getting Miss Flora's prescriptions all filled. Several people had stuck their heads in the door and asked if I had heard the 'not guilty' verdict. Some were standing around inside talking about it all. All of a sudden, four men came walking in and sat down at the corner table. I knew immediately from the way they were dressed they were probably lawyers. They wanted a cup of coffee. I went over and poured them all a cup.

"At first they spoke real low, but the longer they talked, the louder they got. It didn't take long to figure out they were the defense attorneys from the trial. It was obvious they were quite proud of their 'victory' and in no way ashamed of what they had put that poor girl through to achieve it.

"A man had come in unnoticed during all this and had sat down alone at an adjacent table. He was a little man, very modestly dressed. He asked for coffee and quietly drank it without ever looking up. I had been watching him out of the corner of my eye while I watched and listened to the attorneys spouting off.

"I tell you, these guys started to 'what if' that trial to death. They got louder and louder talking about what they would have done 'if' this had happened or 'if' that had happened. You've never seen such cockiness or heard such bragging in your life. It was disgusting to see them sitting there high-fiving each other and making such public spectacles of themselves. Where was the compassion for a poor girl who had been badly wronged? It took all I had not to go over there and shut them up."

My dad got this great look of satisfaction on his face as he continued. "Man, I wish you could have seen what happened next. All of a sudden, that little man got up and walked over to that table of lawyers. They all stopped with their carrying on and looked up at him. You could have heard a pin drop in there it got so quiet. He put his right hand in the air and balled it into a fist and slammed it down right there in the middle of their table.

"What if?" he asked. "WHAT IF?" he asked again, this time much louder. "You want me to tell you about 'what if'? IF WORMS HAD MACHINE GUNS, THEN BIRDS WOULDN'T MESS WITH THEM!!!!!"

"I tell you, I have never seen anything so funny as that fellow wiping the smirks off those lawyers' faces. They sat there looking up at him with their mouths dropped wide open. The little man put the money for his coffee on the table and calmly walked out of the store. Those lawyers never said another word." Dad smiled as he thought of that man putting those hot shots in their place.

"I will never forget that as long as I live. That little man was able to show them for what they were...a bunch of blowhards with no compassion for a tragic situation and no respect for the legal system that fed their families and allowed them to have their expensive suits. I was told later on the girl who had been raped was the man's sister.

"I have thought a lot about what happened today. John, there is a powerful lesson we can learn from this story. Life is full of 'what ifs', Son. You can 'what if' a situation to death. You can waste a lot of time and energy contemplating the 'what ifs', but when all is said and done, they don't mean a thing. What matters is 'what is'. Life is short. You take the cards you are dealt and you make the most of them."

As I told this story to David in the boat that day, I laughed once again as the mental image played over in my head just as it had that day I was twelve years old...these little worms dressed for combat in army fatigues and helmets and holding machine guns...some taking cover behind bunkers, and some standing upright firing at the birds as they swooped down on them.

"You know, David, as a twelve-year old boy, it was impossible to fully grasp what all my dad was trying to teach me with the 'if worms had machine guns' story, but over the years, I have realized how right he was. There was so much to be learned from the little man's reaction in the drug store that day.

"As I got older, I realized Dad was trying to tell me how futile it is to worry about things that haven't come to be. We waste so much time and energy worrying about things that never happen. You can die a thousand deaths from worry. When the trials of life hit, face them head on, deal with them the best you possibly can, but don't borrow trouble, David. Don't 'what if' your life away, Son. Deal with 'what is', deal with your reality. It makes for a happier and more contented life.

"Years later, I realized there was another lesson to be learned from that story. Some would say those lawyers were just doing their job. But you know, Son, there is a time and a place for everything. And in that drug store that day was not the time or place to be celebrating their so-called victory. Always show respect. Those lawyers had no way of knowing the girl's brother was sitting there that day listening to their every word. And that's just the point...you never know who's watching and what effect your actions will have on others. It is important to do your job to the best of your ability, but it is also important to make sure you never compromise your principles or lose your compassion for others. No job is ever worth that. You want to always make sure your conscience is clear when you lie down to sleep at night, Son."

I told David a lot about my father on that fishing trip...how much I wish he could have known his grandfather and how proud he would have been of him.

"Even if I am going to be a lawyer?" David had asked.

"Especially if you are going to be a lawyer, Son. Dad would say the world needs more good, decent, honest and compassionate men out there in the legal profession, and that's just what you will be."

David decided that this would be a good time to take some advice from two very wise men and quit worrying about the 'what ifs'. He would take one day at a time and do the best he could with whatever hand he was dealt.

"Yes, if worms had machine guns, then birds definitely wouldn't mess with them." David smiled as he looked down at his father. "Everything is going to be alright."

No doubt about it.

Life in Montana

"Don't argue with me, David. You've been here two nights now. You need to go home and get some rest."

"It's hard to leave him, Chris."

"I know. Any change at all?"

David motioned for Chris to walk out in the hall with him. "None. And I can tell the doctors were hoping for something more by now.

"Dad has lost a lot of weight. They assure me he is getting all the fluids and nutrients he needs in his IV, but it worries me he hasn't eaten in so long. They are going to insert a feeding tube into his stomach."

Chris shook his head.

"I haven't been able to spend enough time with Charlie. How do you think he's doing?" David asked.

"He's hanging in there. He rode with me to the airport to pick up Aunt Marie and Uncle Sid. They aren't happy with us for waiting this long to tell them what happened. They will be coming to see Dad today."

"I can understand them being upset. But there was no use in interrupting their cruise. There is nothing they could have done but wait. Besides, the whole time Dad was in ICU, we were the only ones they were letting in to see him."

David walked back into the room and over to the bed. He rubbed his dad's shoulders. "I am going to head out of here for awhile, Dad. I

am going to go home and see that little granddaughter of yours. I will
see you later."

Give her a big hug for me, Son.

Chris opened his travel bag and pulled out an old CD he had found
in a storage box at home. "I found this one especially for you, Dad," he
said as he loaded it into the stereo and pushed play.

Nurse Fulton came in. "Hi, Chris. And how are we doing
today?"

"Hello, Nurse Clara. We are glad it's your shift, that's how we are
doing. You need to pass some of that bottle of 'sweet bedside manner'
you have around to the other nurses. I think some of them have been
into the 'sour juice' judging by the scowl on their faces."

Nurse Clara Fulton laughed. "Oh my, your brother said Mr.
Hughes likes all kinds of music, but I wasn't expecting to hear the
rap."

"Well, Dad does like most all kinds of music. He likes pop and
rock and jazz and blues and even some country. But he definitely
doesn't like rap."

"Then I don't understand." Nurse Fulton looked puzzled.

"I figure all that stuff he likes hasn't gotten a response. I thought
I would find the rap CD that caused us the most trouble when I was
a teenager and play it. We will see what kind of response we get from
that. I can assure you if Dad could, he would be telling me to turn
that crap off."

Nurse Fulton laughed. "I see you have your hands full with this
one, Mr. Hughes."

*You don't know the half of it. And yes, Christopher...turn
that crap off.*

"Dad, Charlie and I picked up Aunt Marie and Uncle Sid from the
airport yesterday. They are coming to see you in a little while."

"We'll get you all cleaned up for your company, Mr. Hughes. How
about we get you all bathed and shaved?"

Chris explained to Nurse Fulton that Uncle Sid and Aunt Marie had left for an Alaskan cruise the day before the accident. "They had been looking forward to that cruise for a long time, and David and I decided it was best to wait until they got home to give them the news. We are going to have to hear about it, too."

They have been planning for and looking forward to that cruise for a long time. You boys did the right thing.

It was because of Uncle Sid that I wound up living in Montana and raising my family here.

Mom said she never would have thought in a million years her baby brother would ever leave Georgia. But Uncle Sid called her one day. He was in his junior year of college and Mom had already moved to Illinois and was married. "Guess what, Mary Elizabeth?"

"What's that, Sidney?" she had asked.

"I was in the library today and someone had left a book on the table with pictures of a place they call 'God's country'. Montana, Mary Elizabeth, it's the most beautiful place you ever saw…big majestic mountains, crystal clear rivers and streams, these great big awesome sunrises and sunsets. When I get out of college, that's where I'm going to live. Montana has the biggest, most beautiful blue skies you can imagine, Mary Elizabeth."

"It sounds wonderful, Sidney. But don't you think you should just go for a visit first?"

"I tell you, I am going to live in Montana. That place is calling my name."

Mom said she had laughed and realized her baby brother was as impulsive as she was. "That sounds great, Sidney. When you finish college, please come here to visit J. D. and me for awhile on your way to Montana. I miss you." Mom and Uncle Sid were only eighteen months apart and had always been real close.

"I miss you, too, Mary Elizabeth."

The only thing Uncle Sid ever wanted to do was coach football. He was the quarterback on his high school team and played in college until he messed his knee up. He planned to get a job teaching math somewhere and coach a high school football team. Just as he said he was going to do, after graduation, he loaded up his old Chevy and headed to Montana, making a stop in Illinois for a visit, of course.

"What is your plan when you get there?" Mom asked Uncle Sid as he loaded his car the morning he was leaving for Montana.

"I'm headed straight for the Rocky Mountains, Mary Elizabeth. I plan to see as much as I can, and to just keep on driving. It's a huge place. I'll know when I get where I'm supposed to be."

Mom had reached into the pocket of her house dress that morning and had pulled out three-one hundred dollar bills. "Sidney, you take this. It will come in handy."

"Now, Mary Elizabeth, I'm not going to take your money."

"Yes, you are, Sidney. I will feel much better knowing you aren't out there all alone with no money."

"Thanks, Sis. I will pay you back someday."

"You just take care of yourself. I love you, Sidney."

"I love you, too, Sis. Don't you worry about me. I will be fine. I will let you know where I am once I get settled."

Uncle Sid left that day and headed toward his future in Montana. He traveled straight to the Rocky Mountains as he said he would. He sent Mom a postcard which read, "Mary Elizabeth, those pictures in that book in no way did this place justice. This is the most beautiful place you will ever see. Yes, this is truly God's Country."

He stayed in the mountains for a couple of weeks, and then drove to Missoula, then to Butte, and then to Bozeman.

Uncle Sid looked at his map and decided to head to Billings. About fifteen miles from his destination, he saw a woman standing on the side of the road with a flat tire. He stopped. "Hi ma'am, you need some help?"

"Yes, thank you. I'm glad someone finally came along. My husband has shown me how to change a tire, but I am having some trouble. I would very much appreciate some help. My name is Nora Evans."

"Hi, Mrs. Evans, my name is Sidney Clark."

Uncle Sid noticed Mrs. Evans had walked around the back of his car and had looked at his tag. "I could tell you were a Southern boy when you spoke. I see you are from Georgia. What are you doing in these parts, Mr. Clark?"

"Please, call me Sid." And Uncle Sid began to tell Mrs. Evans what a Georgia boy was doing traveling in Montana as he fixed her flat. He told her about the book in the library. He told her he had just finished college and was going to be a math teacher and a football coach. "I am going to look for a job when I get to Billings."

Mrs. Evans was fascinated. "So, you fell in love with our state by looking at pictures in a book? And you are planning to live and work here? And you don't know a soul?"

"That about sums it up." Uncle Sid realized it all sounded a little crazy when it was put like that. "All finished, ma'am," he said.

"What do I owe you?"

"You don't owe me a thing, Mrs. Evans. I am glad I came along and was able to help you."

Nora Evans knew that having a flat tire and having this polite, sweet, Southern boy come along to fix it was no coincidence. She looked him over. He was tall and athletic. He had brown hair and brown eyes and two of the cutest dimples she had ever seen when he smiled. He looked so young, but no one could deny that this kid had intestinal fortitude.

"Sid, I don't live but a couple of miles from here. Why don't you follow me home? I know my husband would love to meet you. And to thank you, of course."

"Mrs. Evans, really...no thanks necessary. I was glad to help."

"Now, don't argue with me, young man," she said. "Besides, I think you will be more than glad to meet my husband. He just happens to be the principal of the school here, and we just happen to need a math teacher."

Uncle Sid followed Mrs. Evans home that afternoon and met her husband, Randy Evans. He stayed for dinner and they talked until midnight. "Why don't you stay in the guest room tonight?" Mr. Evans had asked him. "We will get up in the morning and eat a good breakfast and show you our little school."

The next morning as they were driving to the school, Mr. Evans had said he couldn't believe the timing of Uncle Sid coming along. "My high school math teacher just let me know last week he wasn't coming back this year. I didn't know what I was going to do."

"What about your football team?" Uncle Sid asked. "I really do want to find a coaching job."

Mr. Evans told Uncle Sid the school was small, but football was big there, and they had been conference champs the past three years. "Coach Wells has been with us for years. He's still got a couple more years before he retires, but if you don't mind an assistant coaching job for now, I'm sure he would love to have some more help."

Mr. Evans showed him around the school. He called Coach Wells to come meet Uncle Sid. Coach Wells and Uncle Sid walked over to the football field and talked for quite awhile. They walked back to the school. "Randy, I like the way this man thinks. I feel sure that he will be a good addition to our school and our football program."

Randy Evans looked at Uncle Sid. "Well, what do you think, Sid?"

"You know, this is a lot to think about. Is it alright if I take a couple of days before I get back to you with a decision?"

"Sure, you take all the time you want," Mr. Evans said.

"Where are you staying?" Coach Wells asked.

"I don't know, you have any suggestions?"

Mr. Evans and Coach Wells looked at each other and laughed. Coach Wells said, "I just happen to know someone who has a nice little bed and breakfast here in town. I think I can get you a decent rate. Why don't you bring him over a little later, Randy?"

Driving back to his house, Mr. Evans explained to Uncle Sid that Coach Wells and his wife had the bed and breakfast. "You will like it there. The food alone is worth going."

That night Uncle Sid had the best meal he had eaten since he had left home. "This is delicious, Mrs. Wells. I haven't eaten anything this good since I left Mama's table."

Mrs. Wells laughed. "I wish I could take the credit, but I can't. You will have to meet my daughter. She is the one who is responsible for these good meals around here. Marie, come in here and meet this nice, young man."

And the rest, as they say, is history. Uncle Sid said once he met someone who could cook as good as Mama, he couldn't let her go. He said it was a bonus that she happened to be so sweet and pretty. Once he met Marie, his decision to stay and take the job at the school was easy to make.

Uncle Sid and Aunt Marie got married. They weren't able to have any children, but Uncle Sid said he had been blessed to have had a small part in shaping the lives of so many students over the years.

Uncle Sid helped Coach Wells take the team to two more conference championships, and five years later, Coach Wells retired and turned the team over to Coach Sidney Clark.

Mom and Uncle Sid kept in close touch. They didn't get to see each other much through the years, but they sent a lot of letters and there were occasional phone calls. Mom sent him my new school picture every year.

When she got sick, she wrote Uncle Sid. "Sidney, could you please plan a visit when school lets out for the Christmas holidays? I am not well, and it's extremely important that we talk."

Uncle Sid came as soon as school was out. He and Mom spent a lot of time in her room with the door shut. Mom seemed more at peace after that visit. I didn't know what they had talked about behind closed doors until many years later. Mom had asked Uncle Sid to please take care of me when she was gone. And Uncle Sid had promised her that he would.

Looking back, I realize how carefully he had approached me that day. He knew how independent I was...how proud, and yes, even stubborn. After all, he knew my mom, and in many ways, I was so much like her.

"What are your plans, John?" Uncle Sid came outside and sat beside me on the deck.

"Plans?" We had just gotten home from my mom's funeral, and this guy is wanting to know my plans? "I just want to be left alone are my plans." I kept my thoughts to myself.

"Yes, John, your plans."

"I don't know. I will be fine. You don't have to worry."

"I know you will be fine, John. It's just your Aunt Marie and I have talked about this and we would love for you to come to Montana and live with us."

"I appreciate the offer, Uncle Sid. But I couldn't impose upon you like that. Besides, my home is here."

Uncle Sid laughed and grabbed me by the shoulders. "Impose? Are you kidding, John? Your mom told me what a good football player you are. Look at how much you've grown since I last saw you. I must admit to you that I have ulterior motives here. I need you on my team. Will you at least think about it?"

I did think about it. There were only a couple of weeks left in the semester. One of Mom's friends had invited me to stay with her and finish the year out at my school. Uncle Sid went home and came back as soon as his school was out for the summer.

I knew going to Montana with Uncle Sid was the right thing to do. I would miss my home and school and friends, but with Mom and Dad gone, nothing was the same anymore. I was just aimlessly going through the motions these days, anyway…just doing the next thing I was expected to do. It really didn't matter where I was. Besides, I knew Mom would want me to go to Montana and live with Uncle Sid.

He picked me up at school. "Last exam over and done, Uncle Sid. I have decided to go back to Montana with you if the offer still stands."

Uncle Sid looked relieved. "Oh, it still stands, John. Aunt Marie will be excited when I let her know you are coming home with me."

Mom and Uncle Sid had met with attorneys when he visited over the Christmas holidays. The legal arrangements had been made and the plans were finalized before Uncle Sid had returned home. The house and store were sold and all debts were paid off. "John, when I was here with Mary Elizabeth, we talked about some things she wanted me to do. She wanted you to have that truck you've been talking about for awhile. When we get home, we will go buy you something to run around in. The rest of the money will be put in a savings account to pay for your college expenses."

I had never met Aunt Marie. Mom had always said that Uncle Sid had a sweet wife. The day Uncle Sid and I drove into his driveway, Aunt Marie came running out and hugged me before she ever hugged Uncle Sid. She immediately made me feel welcome in her home. She told me their home was my home, and I knew she meant it. She was short and plump and so very sweet, and I loved her from the moment I met her.

My aunt and uncle were great. They were there for me during the hard times, and there were many. They understood there were days I needed to talk, and there were days I needed to be alone. They fixed my room up just like the one I'd had back home. They gave me time to adjust and time to grieve. They cried with me when I needed to cry, and they respected my privacy when I needed to have some space.

I was comfortable there. Aunt Marie was a great cook and kept a clean house. She and Uncle Sid loved each other and had a happy home. I was with family. I felt loved and wanted. I knew I was where I was supposed to be.

There was a light knock on the hospital door. "It's okay, come in," Chris said and got up and went to the door. "Did you get some rest? We want to hear all about the cruise."

"Hi Chris." Uncle Sid hugged him. He was visibly upset and had dreaded seeing John this way ever since Chris had told him about the wreck the day before.

Aunt Marie was crying. "I'm sorry…it's just everything you boys have been through. We should have been here with you."

She walked over to the bed. "We love you, John. We are praying for you." Her voice was shaking.

What a sweet lady!

"It's going to be alright, Aunt Marie." Chris put his arm around her. "Dad is tough. He's got these docs scratching their heads around here, right Dad?"

You got that right, Son.

Uncle Sid paced from one side of the bed to the other. "Why did you boys not let us know what happened? We needed to be here with you."

"We talked about it, Uncle Sid. But you had planned to take this cruise after you retired for years. You deserved to have a good time.

If there had been something you could have done…but all we've been able to do is sit around and wait."

"Oh Baby, I am so sorry about your mother." Aunt Marie hugged Chris and was crying again. "We should have been here for you. We should have been with you at the service."

Nikki's service. Oh, Nikki, I can't believe you are really gone.

Cynthia Nicole and the Colonel

I helped Uncle Sid around the school that summer. We painted the gym and locker rooms and got the football field in good shape. I got myself in good shape, too. I ran the track and worked out in the weight room each day when we were finished with our work. It helped to keep my mind occupied and to stay busy.

I was dreading going to a new school for my junior year. I missed my friends. But football practice started on the first day of August, and I got to know the guys on the team. By the time classes started later that month, they considered me 'one of the boys', and it was easier to fit in than I had expected. The school was a little smaller than the one I had come from, but everyone was friendly and also a little curious about this 'new kid on campus'.

The first day of classes, I noticed one girl in particular in my chemistry class. She sat a couple of desks in front of me. She had beautiful blond hair. It was long and straight. When the teacher introduced me to the class, she turned around and smiled. She had gorgeous blue eyes and soft, clear skin. I had never cared much for science, but I knew this would for sure be my favorite class.

The first football game was that Friday night. Uncle Sid had noticed how hard I had worked out all summer. I was much stronger and faster. He had decided to start me at the position of wide receiver, and had asked me to work with the quarterback that first day of practice. His name was Rick Jones.

Rick was the first person I had come into contact with in Montana, and things had not gone well. I had noticed a boy leaning on a bike watching Uncle Sid and me paint the first of the summer. Uncle Sid had waved at him and he had waved back. He moved closer and I finally spoke. "Hi."

"So, I guess since you are the Coach's nephew, you will be getting special privileges around here."

"Whatever." I kept painting. "What a jerk," I had mumbled under my breath that day.

"I heard that."

"Good."

That night when I asked Uncle Sid who the kid was on the bike, he told me he was Rick Jones. "He's my quarterback, and a good one, too."

"He's your quarterback?" I was surprised. "How old is he?"

"He's your age, John. He will be in the eleventh grade, too. I know he's small, but wait until you see him throw a football."

"Oh, swell," I thought.

Rick rode his bike to the school every single day for the next two weeks and just sat there and watched. He watched me paint or cut the grass on the field. He watched me run on the track and even stood in the door of the weight room while I worked out. I ignored him.

"Man, what's your problem?" I had finally asked him.

"I don't have a problem." Rick walked over to me. "I am Rick Jones."

"Yes, I know. I am John Hughes."

Rick apologized for being a jerk earlier. "Yes, I admit it, I was a jerk." He laughed and continued. "It's just that I aim to win the conference this year, and I don't want some new kid who's living with the coach having special privileges on the team and messin' that up."

"Well, I assure you, I will not be getting any special privileges around here. Not from Uncle Sid...I mean Coach Sid...I mean Coach Clark."

They both laughed. They had already become good friends by the time football practice had started. They had worked out together the rest of the summer and Rick knew I had paid the price and deserved to have a starting position on the football team.

The people here were definitely serious about their football. The first game was at home, and the stands were packed. I looked over at the cheerleaders. There she was...the beautiful blond in chemistry class. I had found out her name was Nikki.

I looked up at the game clock. There were ten seconds left in the first half. Rick called the play in the huddle. I went out deep for his pass. I jumped high into the air and caught the ball. On my way down, I was hit like I had never been hit before. I lay motionless on the ground. I opened my eyes. Those gorgeous blue eyes were staring down at me. They looked concerned. "Are you okay?"

It hurt, but I managed a smile. "I will be okay if you say you will go out with me." Did I just say that? The hit must have made me whacky. I had always been shy around the girls. I would never be so forward as to say something like that to someone I didn't even know. "By the way, my name is John."

"Yes, I know," she giggled. "And yes, I will go out with you. But you might change your mind about wanting to go out with me when you meet the 'Colonel'."

"Huh?" I looked around. The team had gathered around to see if I was alright. I raised my hands into the air still holding the ball. The referee signaled a 'touchdown'. Nikki had returned to the sideline with the rest of the cheerleaders.

"Who is the 'Colonel'?"

"I tell you, Man, you don't want to go out with her," Rick was saying. "Yes, she is fine, but no one will go out with her. You had better listen to me, John. Having to deal with the 'Colonel', it's not worth it."

"Well, I disagree. I can't believe you guys are so scared of the man. He can't be that bad."

Cynthia Nicole Jackson, 'Nikki', was the daughter of a retired Colonel of the United States Army. Colonel Robert Walker Jackson had fought in the Vietnam War, and rumor was that he had been captured by the enemy. "He escaped by breaking the necks of his to plead his case. "Come on, John, they say the man is crazy."

Uncle Sid had helped me get a good deal on a used red pickup truck at the local Ford place. Rick had put his bike in the back and had ridden over to Nikki's house with me. I pulled into the driveway of the Jackson home and turned the ignition off.

"Okay, it's your funeral," he said as he got on his bike and pedaled off.

Nikki came running out of the house. "Daddy is expecting you." She giggled. She walked inside her ranch-style home and I followed. We walked through a large kitchen and dining room, then halfway down a long hall.

"This is my room." I had never seen a girl's bedroom before. I stood in the doorway and took it all in. The walls were white with yellow flowers and the bedspread was pink. There were stuffed animals on the bed and a poster of a kitten above a bookshelf. A collection of dolls filled each shelf. Her cheerleader uniform was draped over a chair, and books were strewn on a white desk. A Jackson Browne album was playing on her stereo. The closet door was standing open.

"Are all those clothes and shoes yours?" I asked.

"Yes." She was giggling again. "I need a bigger closet."

"I was thinking you didn't need so many clothes and shoes. You can only wear one outfit or one pair of shoes at a time, you know."

"You guys just don't understand." She was standing close to me and smiling.

I was thinking how pretty she was. I suddenly realized I was standing in her room. I quickly stepped back into the hall. The last thing I needed was for someone to see me in her bedroom. Besides, I was ready to get this meeting with the 'Colonel' over with.

We walked down the hall. "This is Daddy's study." She knocked on the door.

I stood there for what seemed like an eternity. I looked around and Nikki was gone. I finally heard a gruff voice coming from inside the room. "Come in."

I slowly opened the door. The smell of cigar smoke filled the room. A big, black antique desk took up most of the room. A black leather chair was behind the desk, and it faced the wall. I could see the top

66

half of a bald head visible over the top of the back of the chair. A cloud of smoke billowed into the air. There was a huge oil painting of a man dressed in an army uniform sitting on a white horse on the wall behind the desk. There were two samurai swords hanging on each side of the painting. I noticed the man in the painting held one of the swords in his hand. He had the sword raised high in the air as he sat on the horse. There was an American flag in one corner of the room, and the flag of the state of Montana in the adjacent corner. There was a gold plate on the frame of the painting. I squinted my eyes to read it…'Colonel Robert Walker Jackson, U. S. Army, and his Faithful Stallion, Montana.'

"You still have time to get out of here, Boy." The voice was deeper and even gruffer than before.

I looked again at the painting and the swords hanging on the wall. I thought of what Rick had told me earlier. "Maybe I should get out of here while the getting is good," I thought to myself. My legs were shaking. It felt like there was a big knot in my throat keeping me from swallowing. I took a step toward the door. "No, John." My dad's words suddenly came to mind. "Don't ever let anyone intimidate you, Son. Besides, their bark is usually much worse than their bite. Stand your ground. And whatever you do, never let them see you sweat." I wiped the sweat that had formed on my forehead.

The chair started to squeak as the 'Colonel' slowly turned around to face me. He was totally bald on the top of his head, and the little bit of hair he still had that circled the side of his head was completely white. It was obvious he was the same man in the painting, just older and heavier. His brow was wrinkled. His face was red and seemed to grow redder the longer he looked at me.

"Introduce yourself, John. Greet everyone with a handshake and a smile." Dad's words were playing in my head again. I held my hand out to Nikki's father. "I am John David Hughes, Jr., Sir. It's nice to meet you, Colonel Jackson."

"Sit, Boy." He nodded toward a small little folding chair leaning against the desk.

"I think I will stand, Sir."

"Suit yourself." He put out his cigar in the ashtray on the corner of his desk and began to fire the questions at me. "How old are you?"

"Sixteen, Sir."

"How are your grades?"

"My grades are good, Sir."

"Do you drink, smoke, use drugs?"

"No, Sir, none of the above."

"What are your interests?"

"Football, Sir." I could see the disapproval on his face. I could read his mind. "No jock is going to be taking my little girl out," I imagined the words the 'Colonel' had to be thinking.

"Where are you from, Boy?"

"Near Chicago, Sir."

"A city boy."

"No, Sir, I am from a place not much bigger than here. We lived about thirty miles from the city."

"Who are your parents and what do they do?"

"They are deceased, Sir."

The 'Colonel' seemed momentarily caught off guard. Did I detect a small hint of compassion, or maybe concern? There was a cease fire with the questions for a moment as he studied me closer. "Who are you living with?"

I told him my uncle was the Coach and math teacher at the high school, and I was living with him and his wife.

"Oh, you are that boy Sidney Clark has taken in."

Okay, so he knew my uncle. Everyone liked Uncle Sid. Surely that would help a little.

"Sidney Clark appears to be a good man."

"Yes, Sir, he is a very good man."

The 'Colonel' sat there and continued to look at me. There was a calm about him now. He seemed deep in thought. Suddenly, and without warning, he was standing and pointing and screaming at me. "I know what boys your age have on their mind. You stay away from my daughter, you hear me, Boy?"

My legs were shaking again. I opened the folding chair and quickly sat down. About that time, Nikki burst into the room, all bubbly and smiling. "Isn't he great, Daddy? Can we go out? Please? Pretty please?"

I actually saw the gruff old man smile when his daughter entered the room. The red left his face and his whole demeanor changed. His face and voice softened as he spoke to Nikki. "Hi, Princess. Now, let us finish talking and we will see."

His face began to turn red again as she left the room and he looked back at me. His smile turned into a solemn and stern stare. "I see my daughter is bound and determined to go out with you. You listen to me, and you listen to me good. If you ever do one thing to hurt my baby"…he paused and looked back at the swords hanging on the wall behind him. "Do you get what I am saying to you, Boy?"

I swallowed hard. "Yes, Sir. And Sir…my name is John."

The 'Colonel' called for Nikki to come into his office and he laid the ground rules down to us. We were only allowed to go out in groups, never were we to be off together, just the two of us. He wanted to know where we were at all times, and when he set a time for Nikki to be home, he meant not one minute later.

When I got home that evening, I told Uncle Sid about my meeting with Colonel Robert Walker Jackson. "Uncle Sid, I've never been so scared in my life."

Uncle Sid had laughed and patted me on the back. "Yes, he's quite a character. He called me as soon as you left his place. He had a lot of questions for me, too. I told him not to worry, that you were a good boy. I told him you were very disciplined, made good grades, was highly motivated and well-mannered. I assured him his daughter would be in good hands. He's just being protective of his little girl, John."

We had our first date the following Tuesday night. Rick and I drove to Nikki's house to pick up Nikki and her friend, Kelly. We walked the girls to the truck and opened the doors for them. I was climbing into the driver's seat when I looked at the doorway and saw the 'Colonel' motioning for me to come to him.

"Oh, brother," I thought. "I will be right back. Your dad wants to talk to me," I said to Nikki.

"Where will you be taking my daughter tonight, Boy?"

"We are going to a Jr. High football game, Sir."

"Who is with you?"

"Rick Jones, Sir, Robert Jones' son."

The 'Colonel' stretched his neck to see into the truck. He looked at his watch. "What time will the game be over?"

"It should be over by eight-thirty, Sir."

"You have my daughter home by a quarter until nine."

"Yes, Sir."

"I want you to promise me that you will take good care of my daughter."

I looked the 'Colonel' squarely in the eyes. "Yes, Sir, you have my word, Colonel Jackson."

A Promise Broken

It was February of our senior year and Nikki and I had been dating for over a year. Rick had started dating Linda, and we were all hanging out and spending a lot of time together. We had decided to make the most of our senior year. There would be parties, the prom, the spring dance, the athletic banquet, and graduation would be right around the corner.

When our class rings came in, I gave mine to Nikki and asked her to go steady with me. She wore it proudly around her neck on a gold chain.

The church was having a sweetheart banquet on Valentine's night, and I wanted to make it special. After football season had ended, I had taken a job delivering papers before school, and had saved some money.

Aunt Marie took me shopping. "You look so handsome," she said as she admired the navy blue suit she picked out for me to try on. "This one fits you just right." We went by the florist and she helped me pick out some flowers for Nikki.

Uncle Sid was washing his new black Thunderbird when we got home. "Man, you have her shining, Uncle Sid."

"You know, John, I thought you might like to go pick your girl up in this little baby for the banquet tonight."

Aunt Marie jumped up and down and clapped and Uncle Sid laughed as I danced a jig. "Oh man, Uncle Sid, you are the best." I hugged Aunt Marie and thanked her for her help in picking out the suit and the flowers.

"Man, you look pretty," I said to Nikki as I walked her to the car that night. She was wearing a blue dress that matched her eyes, and she had her hair put up. She thanked me for the flowers and told me I looked quite pretty myself.

"Guys aren't pretty, silly."

She laughed. "Okay, you look quite handsome." We pulled out of her driveway and she moved over closer to me as we got farther away from her house.

"That's better." I held her hand.

We had been going out alone the past couple of months. I didn't see much of the 'Colonel' these days. At times I would notice him watching from the window of his study when I picked Nikki up.

Nikki's mom was at the church when we got there. She had volunteered to be a chaperone and had helped decorate the banquet room and prepare the food. Her name was Lois, and she was a very nice lady. I had always wondered what in the world she had ever seen in the 'Colonel'. She was quiet, but always seemed glad to see me when I came over. She would ask how school was going and what all I had been up to. She loved to bake, and when she found out my favorite cake was a peanut butter cake my mom used to make, she had called Aunt Marie and had gotten the recipe and had made it for me.

She came over to us. "You two look so nice together."

I told Mrs. Jackson that the decorations were great. She pointed us toward the photographer, and told us to be sure to go over and have our picture made before we sat down. The meal was delicious. They served a salad with Thousand Island dressing, roast beef, green beans, rice, and strawberry shortcake for dessert.

After the banquet, everyone was meeting at the park. We told them we would see them later. Nikki and I wanted to be alone. I drove down a little road by the school to our parking spot. I took my jacket and tie off and put them in the back seat. I found a good radio station and put my arm around Nikki and told her again how pretty she looked.

The warnings of the 'Colonel' and my promise to him had not been in my thoughts these past months. I was getting more aggressive when Nikki and I were together, and she was getting more permissive. I leaned over and kissed her on the cheek, then on the lips. "I love you, Nik," I told her between kisses.

"I love you, too, John," she replied as we kissed again.

"I want to be with you so bad, Nik."

"I want to be with you, too, John," she said softly.

"Are you sure, Nik?" I asked nervously.

"Yes, I am sure," she answered, her voice reassuring.

Nikki and I made love for the first time that night and she wanted me to hold her for a long time afterwards. I asked her if she was okay.

"Just keep holding me, John."

We lay there in each other's arms. The radio played and I drifted off to sleep.

"What time is it?"

Her question startled me and I jumped. I looked at my watch. "Oh no, the 'Colonel'. I have to get you home."

It was early May. Things couldn't have been better. I was going with the prettiest girl in school. Our football team had won the conference that year, and I had just gotten the MVP award at the athletic banquet. There were only a couple of weeks left of school. I was exempt from all my exams, and the principal had called me in his office to tell me I was salutatorian of our class.

Nikki and I had a fun summer planned after graduation. We had decided to go to the local college in the fall. Rick and Linda were going there, too. It was only twenty minutes away, and I had applied and gotten an academic scholarship. I planned to try out for the football team.

My only regret was that Mom wasn't there to see it all. I knew how excited she would be for me. I sure did miss her.

I looked for Nikki when I got to school that morning, but she wasn't around. After my first class was over, I found out she wasn't there. I hoped she wasn't sick. Her friend, Kelly, came to my locker. "Nikki wants you to meet her at the park."

I left school and headed that way. "That Nikki," I thought, "wanting to goof off this morning rather than go to school." I wondered what she had planned for us...maybe a drive or maybe just to hang out at the mall. But as soon as I saw her, I knew something was wrong. She started crying and ran to me.

"What's wrong?" I asked.

"John, I'm pregnant."

"Pregnant? Are you sure? Have you been to a doctor?"

"No, I haven't been to a doctor, but yes, I am sure. I have always been regular with my periods."

I didn't know so much about all that period stuff, but I would take her word for it. "Pregnant?" I found the closest park bench and sat down. She sat down beside me.

"Say something, John."

The thoughts were running rampant in my head. *Oh man, the ironies of life. I have had more than my share of them. That Valentine's night, we had felt all grown up. We had ignored all that we had been taught through the years...that we were to abstain from sex until marriage. We had ignored all of the warnings of the potential consequences of sex without protection. None of that applied to us. No, because we knew it all. We were ten feet tall and bullet-proof. We were invincible.*

Yes, we were all grown up that night with adult feelings and desires and actions. And here we were just a few weeks later...two kids...scared and way in over our heads.

"What are we going to do, John?"

"I can't think right now. We need to go to class."

"I can't go to class today."

"I have to get to class, Nikki. Uncle Sid knows I went to school this morning. He will be wondering where I am. I need some time to think. We will talk tonight. You go home and get some rest."

I didn't hear one word in my classes the rest of the day. As soon as the last bell rang for the day, I headed to the weight room. Lifting weights had always helped me get my mind off my problems. But it wasn't helping today. I headed to the track and ran to the point of exhaustion. I dropped to the ground and knelt there with my head down.

"What do I do, God? Please help me." I felt ashamed. I had let Him down. I had let Nikki down. Poor Uncle Sid had taken up for me with the 'Colonel'. He would be so disappointed. I had let myself down. "What about all those big plans you have made for your future, John?

"Oh no...the 'Colonel'...my promise to him to take care of his little girl. The 'Colonel' will have to be told. I AM A DEAD MAN!"

"Who's a dead man?"

I looked up and Uncle Sid was standing there. "Yes, you will kill yourself if you go many more laps like that last one," he laughed as he helped me up. "Let's walk to the gym." He continued to talk as we walked. "You missed your second period class today."

"Yea, Nikki needed to talk to me about something."

"Anything you want to talk to me about, John?" Uncle Sid could read my moods just like my mom always could. We got to his office inside the gym and I sat down in a chair across from his desk. He closed the door and walked around and sat in his chair.

Putting this off wasn't going to accomplish a thing, and I needed some help here. "Uncle Sid, I have messed up."

He leaned forward, looking concerned. "John, you know you can talk to me about anything."

"Nikki is pregnant." The words came out way too loud. I lowered my voice and continued. "We just did it once, Uncle Sid, the night of the Valentine's banquet. I wasn't expecting it to happen and I wasn't prepared. I mean, what I am trying to say, is that I was stupid and didn't use any protection."

Uncle Sid sat quietly and looked intently at me as I rambled on. "Mom always told me to wait until marriage. And Dad said that was best, but he knew sometimes that didn't happen. So, one day when we were closing down the store and Mom wasn't there, he opened up a pack of condoms and showed me how to use them and told me how important it was to always protect myself from diseases and unwanted pregnancies. I knew better, Uncle Sid."

His voice was very calm as he asked, "John, does Nikki's parents know that she's pregnant?"

"No. She just told me this morning. The 'Colonel' is going to kill me, Uncle Sid."

"You go over to Nikki's and pick her up, John, and bring her to the house."

I got more scared the closer I got to her house. "Would I have to face the 'Colonel'? Did he know? What am I going to say to Nikki? Will she be mad I talked to Uncle Sid?"

Nikki met me outside. She was home alone. The 'Colonel' was at his weekly domino game at the VFW, and her mom had left a few minutes before I got there. Nikki got in the truck and turned to me. "John, do you want me to get rid of it?"

"Get rid of it? What do you mean?" Then I realized what she was talking about...an abortion. "Now, wouldn't that be easy and convenient?" I thought sarcastically.

"No!" I answered back, almost in a yell. Trying to lower my voice, I continued, "I mean, no. Yes, the timing sucks, and yes, I wish this hadn't happened...not now. But this is our baby, and just because the timing isn't right doesn't mean I want to make it go away."

"Okay, that sounded mature," I thought to myself. But did I mean it? "Absolutely," I assured myself. "An abortion is totally out of the question."

I continued, "Yes, this is an inconvenience, but this is our son or daughter we are talking about here." I looked over at Nikki. I wanted to see how she had reacted to what I had said. "How do you feel about it, Nikki?"

"Relieved that you feel that way, John."

I hugged her and gave her a light kiss on the lips. "Everything is going to be alright. I told Uncle Sid. He wants to see us at the house."

When we drove up, Mrs. Jackson's car was there.

"Mom's here."

"I see that."

We walked into the living room. Aunt Marie and Mrs. Jackson were sitting on the couch drinking coffee. Uncle Sid got up out of the recliner. He told Nikki to sit in the rocking chair and motioned for me to sit in the recliner he had just gotten up from.

Everyone just sat there. Finally Uncle Sid nodded his head at me. I knew he was telling me to say what needed to be said. Before I could get any words out, Mrs. Jackson spoke. "I have a bad feeling that I'm not here for coffee and chit chat. Nicole, are you pregnant?"

"Yes, Mama." Mrs. Jackson began to cry. Nikki walked over to her. "I am so sorry, Mama." She looked over at me. "We are so sorry."

My dad's words came rushing to me as I stood up to move closer to Nikki and her mom. "Don't be in such a hurry to grow up, John. There is plenty of time for that later." *How I wish I had listened, Dad. How I wish I had kept my word to the 'Colonel'. What do I do now?*

"Mrs. Jackson, I am so sorry." I looked over at Aunt Marie. I needed her and Uncle Sid to know how sorry I was, too.

I kept hearing my dad's words speaking to me. "When the cards are dealt, you have to play your best hand, Son." More of his words flashed in my head. "Whatever pitch life throws your way, you step back, you take your best swing, and you knock that sucker right out of the park."

I will, Dad. I will step up to the plate. I will make you proud.

I walked over to Nikki and took her hand. We walked over to the fireplace. I put my arm around her and began to speak. "We have made a big mistake, and we are so sorry to have hurt and disappointed you. But we want to do the right thing. We have talked about it, and an abortion is out of the question. We just need some time to figure out what we are going to do."

Nikki began to cry and I tried to comfort her.

Mrs. Jackson spoke, "Well, first thing, Nicole, we need to get you to a doctor."

Aunt Marie spoke next. "Graduation is just a couple of weeks away. What do you think about you two trying to concentrate on winding up your senior year and getting your diplomas, then we can make more plans after that."

Mrs. Jackson agreed.

Was I the only one who had it on his mind? "The 'Colonel'…what about the 'Colonel'?" I asked.

Everyone looked at Mrs. Jackson. "You leave the 'Colonel' to me."

I am a dead man!

A Wedding

Nikki's mom took her to the doctor the following day. She was definitely pregnant. The doctor said everything looked good.

We all met again at Uncle Sid's after graduation. Mrs. Jackson had decided it was time to tell the 'Colonel'. Nikki was having morning sickness and he was beginning to ask questions.

I insisted that I should be the one to tell him, but everyone thought that was a bad idea. I wondered if they all had the same thoughts I did…thoughts of those swords on the wall and thoughts of my head on a silver platter.

I had officially asked Nikki to marry me the night of graduation. "What do you think we are having?" I asked her as I rubbed her stomach.

"I think it's going to be a boy," she said.

"Oh yea? I say it's either going to be a boy or a girl."

"Well, I should hope so."

We laughed. It had been awhile since we had laughed. Nikki went on to say that if it was a boy, she wanted to name him John David Hughes, III. "And I want to call him David."

"I like that," I told her.

We decided to have a small wedding ceremony at the end of June. Mrs. Jackson insisted that we have it at the Jackson home. We told her and Uncle Sid and Aunt Marie of our plans to get a small apartment close to campus. I was going to get a job and start college for the fall semester.

Mrs. Jackson said it sounded like we had a good plan in place. "Well, I'll be going," she said. "Nicole, it's time to tell your father."

Mrs. Jackson never told me what all was said that day, but I know it didn't go well. I kept insisting that I needed to go talk to the 'Colonel', but was told over and over again by Nikki and her mom that it wasn't a good idea. They said it was best to stay clear for now.

I called and Mrs. Jackson answered the phone. "How is Nikki doing?"

"She's fine, John. It's just hard for her right now. She and her father have always been so close. He's hurt, and well, it's going to take some time."

"Mrs. Jackson, I need to come over and talk to him. I can't keep avoiding him forever."

"I understand that, John. But please trust me on this. Give it some time. He will come around, but right now, nothing good would come out of you and Bob being in the same place."

I did as I was told, but it was against my better judgment. I knew what the old man was thinking. The thought of the 'Colonel' thinking I was afraid to face him was making me crazy. Okay, so I was afraid… or maybe a better word was terrified…

Uncle Sid and I let the girls do all the planning and getting ready for the wedding. They told us we would just get in the way. It suited us just fine to let them handle all the tedious details. He rode with me to the college to look for apartments and to put in some job applications.

"It's going to be tough for awhile, John," he told me. "Going to college…all the studying it requires, holding down a job, adjusting to having a wife and a new baby…there won't be much time for sleeping."

"I know, Uncle Sid. But we will make it."

"I know you will, John. I'm glad you will only be twenty minutes away. You know Aunt Marie and I will want to help you out with the baby some."

It seemed the perfect time to tell him how much I appreciated everything he and Aunt Marie had done for me. I thanked him for taking me in and treating me like a son. I also thanked him for standing by me during this time. I told him I never meant to embarrass him or our family name.

"Nonsense, John. We all make mistakes. Your Aunt Marie and I are real proud of the way you have handled this whole situation."

Nikki came over to eat with us that night. We sat on the swing on the front porch and talked. I told her about a couple of apartments we had seen that looked promising. "Nothing fancy, Nik, and small, but close to the campus and something we can afford." I told her about the places I had applied for work. We decided to drive over in a couple of days and put a deposit down on one of the apartments.

She told me how the wedding plans were coming along. She said that she and her mom and Aunt Marie were going shopping the following day for her wedding dress.

I was helping Uncle Sid change the oil in his truck.

"The phone is ringing, John. Can you go answer it?"

"Sure," I said, wiping my hands with a rag. I went inside the kitchen. "Hello?"

"This is Colonel Robert Walker Jackson. I need to see you in my study ASAP." The 'Colonel' had hung the phone up before I could answer him.

"Uncle Sid, sorry, but I have to be somewhere." I didn't slow down as I walked past him to my truck. I didn't want to have to answer any questions. I wanted to get over there as fast as I could. I could feel the adrenalin pumping through my body. I was driving way too fast. I suddenly slowed down. Nikki and her mom and Aunt Marie were shopping for the wedding dress. We would be alone. "No time for fear now, John," I said aloud. "Just go in there and get this over with."

The front door was ajar. I walked inside the house and down the hall. The door to the study was always closed. Today it was standing wide open. "Colonel Jackson?"

There was no response. I took a couple of steps inside. "Colonel Jackson?" I sat in the folding chair and waited.

The black leather chair was again turned toward the wall. The chair began to squeak just as before as he turned to face me. I saw the eyes of a madman looking at me. I heard the words bellowing from his mouth. "THERE WILL BE NO WEDDING!"

We sat in silence. He finally continued, "We both know you can't take care of my little girl and a baby. Here's your chance, Boy. You take off running like the yellow-bellied-no-good-for-nothing scoundrel that you are. I will make sure they are well taken care of."

"No, Sir."

"Boy, don't you get it? I am letting you off scot-free. You get out of our lives forever and you can get on with whatever it is you do. You never have to bother with us again. I am talking about all this responsibility and worry off your back. Now, that's quite an offer, Boy."

"I said no Sir, Colonel Jackson. I love your daughter and I will be a good husband to her and a good father to my child. It will be hard at first, and I know right now it's just words, but you will see."

"Boy, you are a bigger fool than I thought." The 'Colonel' started laughing. His laugh made my skin crawl. "Very well, then. It will be a pleasure to sit back and watch you fall flat on your face. And I will be here, waiting and watching. I will be the first one to pick up the pieces and the first one to tell you I told you so. You may go now, Boy."

"Yes, Sir. And it's not Boy. My name is John."

I never told anyone about that meeting with the 'Colonel' that day. And irony of all ironies, it wound up being the 'Colonel's' words that kept me motivated, no matter how tough the going got. *I will show that ole crazy SOB.*

We put a deposit down on the apartment Nikki liked best, and got it decorated with furniture that Aunt Marie and Mrs. Jackson had given us. It was small, a one bedroom, so there wasn't room for much. We had a bed and dresser in the bedroom, a couch and chair and television in the den, my stereo, and a small kitchen table with a couple of chairs in the kitchen.

I moved into our new place that following weekend to start my jobs. I was hired to work full time at the grocery store across the street from the apartment. My hours there were from seven in the morning until four in the afternoon, with an hour off for lunch. After that, I had an hour to shower and change and get ready for my job waiting tables at the restaurant. My hours there would be from five to ten. I had talked to one of the guys there who said his tips were pretty good at times.

Nikki wanted to stay at the apartment, too, but I told her it wasn't a good idea until after the wedding. It had been bad enough when word had gotten around our small community that she was pregnant. We sure didn't need everyone knowing we were living together, too.

"So, since when do you care what people think?" she asked.

"Since now," I said as I winked at her.

The wedding was on the last Sunday afternoon of June. I had worked at the restaurant until almost eleven the night before, and had gotten back to the apartment and tried to sleep, but had tossed and turned all night. Just about the time I drifted off to sleep, the alarm went off. I woke up feeling jittery. It felt like butterflies were in my stomach. It was my wedding day.

I showered and put on some jeans and a t-shirt. I put on some music and ate a bowl of cereal.

"Oh man, Nikki will be with me here tonight," I thought. I wanted to clean the place up a bit. I washed the dishes and swept and mopped the floor. I cleaned the bathroom and put out fresh towels. I looked at the bed. I had slept alone my whole life. Starting tonight, I would be sharing the bed with my wife. Those words sounded strange. "My wife. My wife. My wife." I said them over and over again. I stripped the sheets off the bed and put the light blue set on that Aunt Marie had given to us. I put the white bedspread on and tried to keep all the sides even. It didn't look as good as when Aunt Marie did it, but it wasn't bad.

When everything looked in place, I turned off the stereo, locked up, and headed to Uncle Sid's. I was glad we had planned for a small ceremony. I couldn't imagine what a mess I would be if we were having a big church wedding. This was bad enough. I hated being so nervous. I would be so glad for it to all be over. I thought about Nikki and wondered how she was feeling this morning.

I had decided to wear my navy suit. Nikki liked the way it looked on me. I put on the navy pants and a white shirt and white tie and decided I would wait until right before the ceremony to put on the jacket.

The house looked nice. There were flowers everywhere and candles lit. The guest list was small. Uncle Sid, Aunt Marie, Rick, Linda, and Kelly were there. The preacher was there, and Nikki's mom, of course. "Where's the 'Colonel'?" I asked Mrs. Jackson.

"He won't be here. He went out of town yesterday. He said he didn't want any part of it. It hurts Nikki that her dad won't be at her wedding, but I talked to her, and explained to her that for now, it is best he's not here. She understands that, but I know she wishes things were different."

I walked outside. I felt so bad. Nikki and her father had been so close, and now, because of me, they weren't even speaking. Here she was getting married without her father's blessing.

Mrs. Jackson followed me outside. "John, don't let this spoil your day." She hugged me and told me she wished all the best for Nikki and me in our new life together. She said she would always be here for us and to let her know if there was ever anything she could do to help.

I thanked her and kissed her on the cheek.

"He'll come around, John."

The next few months were hectic, to say the least. I worked the two jobs and Nikki got a job as a receptionist. When classes started for the fall semester, I quit the job at the grocery store and kept the job waiting tables at night. Some nights I would fall asleep sitting at the kitchen table with a book in my hands. I was determined to make good grades and keep my academic scholarship.

Nikki worked until mid-October. She was eight months pregnant and miserable. I insisted she go to her mom's some during the week. Between going to class and working and studying, I wasn't very good company. She was lonesome in our little apartment.

Mrs. Jackson called early one Sunday morning and invited us to come there for lunch. "Both of you come, John. I haven't seen you in awhile."

I told Nikki she should go, but I felt it best if I didn't. I knew I would be the last person the 'Colonel' would want to sit with at Sunday lunch. "I will go to Uncle Sid's," I told her.

I drove Nikki to her home, and before I could pull out of the driveway, Mrs. Jackson came out. "Please come in, John."

I noticed there were only three plates set at the table. No one said anything as Mrs. Jackson fixed a plate and took it to the 'Colonel' in his study. We sat down to eat and Mrs. Jackson blessed the food. It was good to have a big meal of roast and corn and peas and creamed potatoes and homemade rolls. She smiled as I reached for a second helping of everything.

"This is delicious, Mrs. Jackson."

"Save some room now, John," she said. "I have made a peanut butter cake. What you don't eat, you can take home with you. And there is something we need to talk about."

I stopped eating and looked at her. "Yes, Ma'am?"

"Enough of this Mrs. Jackson. You are my son-in-law now."

"What shall I call you?"

"Whatever you please, John."

I thought about it for awhile. I asked her what she wanted her grandchildren to call her. "Well, we used to call my grandmother 'Mimi', and I liked that."

"Then would it be alright if I call you Mimi?"

My mother-in-law smiled and said, "That would be wonderful."

We stopped by Uncle Sid's and visited with him and Aunt Marie on the way back to the apartment. That became our Sunday routine. The 'Colonel' stayed hidden away in his study as we ate our lunch. Each time we got ready to leave, I would ask Nikki, "Are you going to go in to see your daddy before we leave?"

Her answer was always the same. "Not today."

I had not seen the 'Colonel' since the day he told me there would be no wedding. But I knew he was doing just what he said he was going to do…he was waiting and watching.

It was the middle of November. The doctor said it would be any day now. We decided it best for Nikki to stay full time at her mom's until the baby came so she wouldn't be alone.

I had just gotten home from class and called her. She was so ready for this to be over. I knew she was miserable. It was getting harder for her to get around.

"Oh yea," she said, her voice pepping up a bit. "Things are a little better with Daddy and me."

"That's good, Nik." I knew that meant a lot to her.

"Remind Mimi to call me just as soon as the labor starts."

"John?"

"What is it, Nikki?"

"Can you come now?"

"Nikki?"

"My water just broke. The baby is coming." She hollered to her mom that it was time to go to the hospital.

"I love you. I am on my way."

"He'll Come Around"

"You are going to wear holes in your shoes, John."

"I can't help it, Uncle Sid. What could be taking so long?"

Uncle Sid laughed. "Be patient. Babies come when they are good and ready, and not one minute before."

"You know, Uncle Sid, I always heard people say they didn't care what they had, as long as everything went okay and it was healthy. I sure know what they were talking about now."

"There comes your Aunt Marie."

"Aunt Marie?"

"How would you like to come meet your baby boy, John?" she asked as she hugged me.

"A boy? Did you hear that, Uncle Sid? I have a baby boy!"

"Congratulations, John," Uncle Sid said with a big grin on his face.

"Is everything alright with Nikki and the baby?"

"Yes, John. Nikki is doing well, she's just real tired. And that little boy is a fine one. He weighs eight pounds and has a head full of dark, thick hair. I noticed right away how much he looks like your baby pictures."

Aunt Marie and I walked to the hospital room. I stopped and took a deep breath and then walked inside. Nikki was lying in the bed. I looked around the room. "Where is he?"

Nikki smiled. She looked tired. "The nurse is getting him cleaned up and checked out. She said she would have him back in just a few minutes. He is beautiful, John. Wait until you see him. He looks just like his daddy."

I leaned over and kissed her. "How are you feeling?"

"I am so glad this is over. And so relieved that everything went well and we have a healthy baby."

"Where's Mimi?" I asked.

Aunt Marie laughed. "Are you kidding me? She was step for step with that nurse. She wasn't about to let that grandson of hers out of her sight."

"Good for her," I said.

Uncle Sid was standing at the door. I motioned for him to come in. "We are going to name him John David Hughes, III, and call him David."

"David is a fine name," Uncle Sid said.

The nurse came back in the room with the baby. "Are you the proud papa?"

"Yes." I was nervous. "And I have never held a baby before. Please make sure I do it right."

She laughed and placed him in my arms. "You will do just fine."

I looked at my little boy for the very first time. "Oh, my goodness, I didn't know a baby could be this beautiful!" Tears were streaming down my face. I studied every square inch of my boy. I counted his ten fingers and his ten toes. "He's absolutely perfect, Nik. You did good." I walked over to the bed so she could see our son again.

"WE did good, John."

"Yes, you two did make a pretty baby." Mimi was back in the room and beaming over her new grandson.

I have tried many times over the years to explain the feeling that came over me the first time I held my first-born son, and I still to this day can't find the words. I just know that at that moment, everything about my life made sense. I found meaning and purpose to my existence. All the sacrifices seemed worthwhile.

I leaned down and kissed my son on his forehead. I spoke quietly in his little ear. "Welcome to the world, Little Guy. I am your dad and

I love you so much. This is all new to me, but I promise I will be the best dad to you I can possibly be. And I promise I will always be here for you."

The next three weeks were difficult, to say the least. I had my first college exams coming up, but all I wanted to do was to spend time with my little boy.

We decided that Nikki and the baby should stay at Mimi's until after the holidays were over. We set a bassinet up in her bedroom. Mimi assured me she would take good care of them. I told Mimi I knew they would be fine, but it was going to be hard being away from them and trying to concentrate on my studies.

"You just get through those exams, John. Then you plan to stay here with us through the holidays."

I talked to Nikki about her mom's offer. "I don't know if that's such a good idea."

"John, I think you should plan to stay here. Mama wouldn't have offered if she didn't think it would be okay. And if he doesn't like it, then that's his problem."

"I just don't want to upset him here at holiday time. But I do want to be with you and David."

The next three weeks couldn't pass fast enough for me. I went to class each day and then to the restaurant. As soon as I got off work each night, I would go to the apartment and sit at the kitchen table and study until I could no longer stay awake. I made short visits to see my wife and son every chance I got.

When my final exam was over, I worked my shift at the restaurant and headed straight to Nikki's parents' to spend my first night with my son. Nikki was already asleep when I got there. Mimi was sitting in the den rocking David.

"He's such a sweet baby," she said as she handed him to me. "How did you do on your tests?"

"I think I did just fine on them. Oh, Mimi, I have been counting the hours until I could be here with this boy. How has Nikki been doing?"

"She's fine. She's been sleeping a lot. I told her she had better take advantage of this time. Once you all get settled back at the apartment, she will not have much time for sleeping."

I looked down at my son. I looked over at Mimi. "I can't get over how beautiful this baby is." I looked back down at him. This time David's face was wrinkled and he was beginning to get fussy. "Well, I have wanted a lesson in changing diapers, and it looks like this is the perfect time for that lesson."

"Come on, John, let's get him changed."

"I didn't know a little guy could make such a big mess."

Mimi laughed. "Oh yea, that's something babies are quite good at from the start. You will be amazed at how many diapers he will go through in a day."

Mimi took me to the kitchen and showed me how to fix his bottle. She explained why the milk had to be heated, and how important it was to test it on my arm before I gave it to him. She watched as I fed him and showed me how to burp him when he was finished with it.

David went to sleep and we decided we had better get some sleep, too. I told Mimi goodnight and took him to the bedroom. I lay him down in the bassinet and went into the bathroom and took a quick shower. I got some boxers and a t-shirt out of my suitcase and put them on. I lay down next to Nikki and looked at the clock on the nightstand. It was already after midnight. It felt strange sleeping in her old bedroom. It felt even stranger sleeping under the same roof as the 'Colonel'. I knew he had to be quite unhappy knowing I was there. I had seen him looking out the window of his study when I drove up. "Yes, I'm sure he's seething in there," I thought. I was tired. I drifted off to sleep.

David was crying. I looked at the clock. It was almost two-thirty. "Nikki, the baby is crying."

"Its okay, Mama will get up with him."

"Your mom has been getting up with him every night?" I sat up in the bed.

"Yes, she doesn't mind." Nikki rolled over and went back to sleep.

Mimi was standing at the door. "You go back to sleep, John. I know you are worn out."

"No, Mimi, you go back to bed. I will get up with him." I got out of bed and went to the bassinet. "You are soaking wet, Little Man. That milk goes right through you, I see." I picked David up and carried him to the den. "There, all done," I said as I finished changing his diaper.

I walked into the kitchen and Mimi was already getting his bottle ready. "I figured he would sleep longer than this," I said to her.

"Now you see why we keep saying you won't get much sleep. He will be waking up needing changing and feeding every couple to three hours for awhile. But keep the faith. Thankfully, that doesn't last long. It just seems like forever." She grinned.

We went into the den. I sat in the rocking chair and gave David his bottle. "This is such a great room, Mimi." The den was cozy. There was a big fireplace, and the rocking chair was perfect for feeding and rocking a baby to sleep.

"I spent many hours in this room and in that very chair rocking Nicole to sleep when she was a baby."

"You go back to bed, Mimi. David will be asleep again soon, and we won't be far behind you."

"Alright, goodnight, boys," she said as she went back to bed.

"You have a good grandmother, David. I wish Mom could be here to see her first grandchild. You know, Son, your first Christmas is just a few days away. My mom used to sing Christmas carols to me during the holiday season. Let's see...like this one." I very quietly started singing 'Joy to the World'. David smiled at me. "Oh, you like it when I sing to you?"

There was a mirror above the fireplace. I saw the reflection of someone standing in the doorway behind me. It was the 'Colonel'. He was standing there in red and white checked boxers and a white t-shirt. I wondered how long he had been standing there.

I looked down at David. He was asleep. I looked back at the mirror and the reflection was gone. I took David back to his bed and got into mine. I was asleep before my head hit the pillow.

The same scenario played out each day and night until Christmas. Classes were over and I was able to pull double shifts at the restaurant. With everyone in the holiday spirit, the tips were generous and the extra money would come in handy. I worked until ten every night, and then drove the twenty minutes or so back to Mimi's.

David continued to wake up on schedule during the night, but I now heard him as soon as he stirred, and was up before he cried and woke anyone up. Some nights I was so tired until I went to sleep in the rocking chair before he did. But I loved those special times…just me and my son.

I would change him and give him his bottle and talk to him and sing to him. And each night like clockwork, the 'Colonel's' reflection could be seen in the mirror. He would just stand there and observe. I made the decision to pretend he wasn't there. I didn't like being there anymore than he liked having me there, but since my son and my wife were there for the holidays, we would just have to make do the best we could. And I felt it best to ignore the old man. "We will be out of your hair soon," I thought. I looked up again and he was gone.

It was Christmas Eve. I stopped at a flower shop on the way to work and bought a poinsettia plant for Uncle Sid and Aunt Marie and one for Mimi. I had bought a red sweater for Nikki the week before. With David growing so fast, we thought it best to get him clothes for his first Christmas. I was paying for the plants and noticed a shelf lined with stuffed animals. I saw a cute little brown puppy with big, floppy ears. "Can you please wrap this up for me?"

While David's puppy was being wrapped, I looked around the store. I saw a big coffee mug. It was white and had an American flag on it. It had the words 'I LOVE MY GRANDPA' written on it in red. I picked up the mug and then put it back down.

The lady came from the back of the store with the puppy gift-wrapped. "Will there be anything else for you?"

I picked the mug up again. "Yes, could you please wrap this for me, too?"

I worked until eleven that night. We had several Christmas Eve parties and the restaurant had been much busier than usual. I was excited about David's first Christmas. He was only five weeks old and wouldn't know what was going on, but I was still excited about it.

It was late, but the 'Colonel's' light was still on in his study when I drove into the driveway. I reached across the seat for the mug. The lady at the flower shop had wrapped it in red paper and had put a white bow on top. I found a pen and wrote on the card, 'Merry Christmas, Grandpa. I love you. Your Grandson'.

Mimi had given me a key to the house. I unlocked the front door and walked down the hall to the study. I knocked lightly on the door.

"Yes?"

I opened the door just enough to put the Christmas present inside the door on the floor. "Merry Christmas, Colonel," I said through the crack in the door. I quietly shut the door and went to check on David. He and Nikki were sound asleep.

I went back to the truck and got the puppy and the sweater and put them under the bed. I made another trip outside and brought the poinsettias in. Aunt Marie and Uncle Sid were coming over for Christmas dinner, and I would give theirs to them then.

I showered and got into bed. I heard David beginning to stir. I got out of bed and picked him up. "Merry Christmas, Little Man." He smiled at me.

I changed his diaper and walked with him to the kitchen to fix his bottle. I walked to the den and over to the Christmas tree. "Look how pretty, David. Santa Claus has already come. See all your presents?" I sat in the rocking chair and gave him his bottle. "You are a good boy. Santa was good to you, Son."

I started singing to him. He continued to smile as I sang. I sang 'Jingle Bells', then 'I Saw Mommy Kissing Santa Claus', then 'Silent Night'.

"My mama used to sing those songs to me." I jumped. The 'Colonel' was standing in the doorway. I turned around. He was walking into the room. He sat down in the chair across from us. "You've been working some long hours this week."

"Yes, Sir. The tips have been good. People seem to be more generous during the holidays."

"You aren't getting much sleep."

"I don't mind. I enjoy my time with my Little Man."

The 'Colonel' got up out of his chair and walked across the room. He looked at me and then at David. "He's a fine one."

"Yes, Sir, he is."

"Well, I had better get to bed. I wanted to thank you for my Christmas present. I mean, I wanted to thank my grandson. Goodnight."

"Goodnight, Colonel."

I took David back to the bedroom and put him to bed. I lay down and thought about my encounter with the 'Colonel'.

Did that really just happen? Man, John, you must be more sleep-deprived and tired than you even knew. Surely you were dreaming.

I went to sleep.

"What time is it?" I asked.

Nikki was sitting on the side of the bed holding David. "It's early. Why don't you go back to sleep?"

"I will, but first…" I reached under the bed and got the presents I had put under there the night before. "Merry Christmas, you two."

Nikki lay David down beside me and came over to my side of the bed. She leaned over and kissed me. "Merry Christmas, John." She opened her red sweater. "It's beautiful; I am going to wear this today."

"YOU are beautiful," I told her as I kissed her again. I moved over in the bed so she could lie down beside me. I put my arms around her. "You know what I want for Christmas?" I asked her.

"Yes, I do." She smiled. "Patience, John. It won't be much longer. We have our six weeks check-up next week, and I'm sure we will get the go-ahead then."

"It's hard to be patient with you looking this good on Christmas morning, you know." I laughed and kissed her again. "Okay, then you might as well open this for David." I picked him up and lay him on my chest. "Our first Christmas together…"

"Oh, what a cute puppy. Look at what your daddy got you, David. I'll be right back."

"Open it," she said, as she walked back into the bedroom and handed me the present she had bought me for Christmas.

I sat up in bed and opened the present and held up the white shirt and blue sweater that was inside. "I love it. Thanks, Nik. And I will wear this today."

"I want you to lie down and get some sleep this morning, John. David and I are going to see what's going on in the kitchen."

I went back to sleep and slept for most of the morning. When I woke up, I felt rested. I showered and put on some jeans and my new white shirt and blue sweater. I was hungry.

I heard Uncle Sid's voice as I walked to the kitchen. "Merry Christmas, everyone. It smells great in here," I said.

Mimi was cooking turkey and dressing. Aunt Marie had baked a ham and had fixed peas and corn and beans. I smelled homemade rolls baking in the oven.

We all sat down at the dining table. As always, the 'Colonel's' place at the end of the table was empty. Mimi fixed his plate and took it to him in the study. When she got back, she asked everyone to hold hands and asked Uncle Sid to bless the food. Uncle Sid thanked God for all the many blessings He had given our family, and he thanked Him especially for our new addition to the family. I squeezed Nikki's hand. He thanked God for the wonderful meal we were about to share and thanked Him for Christmas and for sending His Son to die on the cross for us all. He prayed for a good new year ahead for each of us. It was a wonderful prayer and we all said 'Amen'.

I opened my eyes and saw the 'Colonel' standing at the end of the table holding his plate. Nikki got up and went over to him and hugged him. "Merry Christmas, Daddy."

"Merry Christmas, Princess." He sat down in his chair. "Hello, everyone. Welcome. Let's eat."

After the 'Colonel' had finished eating, he got up from the table and headed back to his study. Uncle Sid smiled and winked at me.

Nikki looked at her mom and shrugged her shoulders. "This is delicious, Mama."

"Yes, it is," everyone agreed.

All of a sudden, the 'Colonel' was standing back at the table. He had the mug in his hand. "I wanted you all to see what my grandson gave me for Christmas." He passed it around the table for everyone to see. "This is the best present I have ever gotten."

"I can see why, Bob," Mimi said as she examined the mug and read the card folded up inside it. She was trying to hold back her tears of joy, but wasn't being very successful.

Mimi and Aunt Marie went into the kitchen to bring out the pies and cakes they had made for dessert.

When the mug got back around to the 'Colonel', he poured the remaining tea from his glass into it and raised it high. "Merry Christmas, everyone."

I was sitting next to the 'Colonel'. He leaned over to me. "Merry Christmas, to you, John."

"Merry Christmas, Colonel."

Grey Clouds on Sunny Days

It was Memorial Day. Uncle Sid was grilling hamburgers in the back yard. Aunt Marie and Mimi were in the kitchen preparing the baked beans and potato salad. Rick and Linda were coming over. David was laughing as the 'Colonel' and I passed him back and forth between the two of us.

"He's a fine one, John," the 'Colonel' said.

"Yes, he is, Colonel. Good genes," I replied.

"On which side?" the 'Colonel' countered.

"Why, both sides, of course."

"Good answer." We both laughed and David laughed with us.

I had just completed my sophomore year of college and we had just gotten back to Uncle Sid's after moving into a bigger apartment. Uncle Sid and Rick and I had moved all the furniture and Aunt Marie and Mimi and Linda and Nikki had decorated David's new bedroom.

It would be good to have more space and to have the two bedrooms. It had been cramped having David's baby bed in the small hallway between the bedroom and the bathroom.

David was eighteen months now. The 'Colonel' had stayed behind during the move and had kept him entertained. "He is the little boy that Bob always wanted," Mimi would say. "He is keeping him young."

Mimi came out of the kitchen with a pitcher of iced tea and put it on the picnic table. "Those hamburgers smell great, Sid. You can't beat a good grilled hamburger."

"I have to agree with you, Lois. And these are just about ready."

Mimi looked over at her husband. He was tickling David and passing him back to John. David laughed as he made the sound of an airplane taking off and passed him back into his father's arms. She thought about that first Christmas with David. She had snuggled especially close to her husband that night when they got in bed.

"You made me so happy today, Bob. When you came to our Christmas table and sat down and ate dinner with us... that was the best gift you could have ever given me."

"I was wrong about that boy, Lois," he had told her. "I am usually a pretty good judge of character, but I never gave him a chance. I assumed the worst from the start."

The 'Colonel' had paused and continued. "I've been keeping an eye on him. That boy is going to college and making good grades. He is working and supporting his family. I've seen him sitting up with his son all hours of the night taking care of him this week when he had to be past going. But he never complained. And have you noticed how good he is to our little girl and our grandson?"

"Yes, he's a good boy, Bob."

"That's just it...he's still a kid...a teenager. I've seen him show more maturity and responsibility this week than most men twice his age ever show. Now, that's character, Lois. That's the kind of man who I was proud to have serve under me. And that's the kind of man who I am proud to have for a son-in-law.

"I'm a stubborn man, Lois; you know that better than anyone. But I can admit to you here and now that I misjudged him. Yes, John is a good boy."

Mimi looked over at Nikki. She sat alone in a lawn chair, totally disinterested in her surroundings. She walked over to her. "What's wrong, Honey?"

"Nothing, Mama," she said.

Rick and Linda had just driven up. "You guys are just in time," Uncle Sid said as he took the last of the hamburgers off the grill.

The 'Colonel' and I were sitting on the grass under the big oak tree rolling a ball to David. I got up and went over to say hello to Rick and Linda. "It's about time you two got here."

Linda laughed and proudly stuck out her hand. "Is this an excuse for being late?"

"Is that an engagement ring I see?" I looked over at Rick and he winked at me. I had gone with him to the jewelry store a few days before when he purchased the ring.

"Linda is the one, John," he had said to me that day. "And this is the ring. I want to get married the summer after we graduate."

I walked over to where Nikki was sitting. "Come see the engagement ring that Rick has given to Linda."

Nikki mumbled that she would see it later and continued to sit in the chair. I walked back to where Rick and Linda were standing. "She will see it later. She isn't having a good day. I am going to help the girls bring the food outside. It's time to eat."

Linda rolled her eyes at Rick. "When does she ever have a good day?" she had asked him as John walked away to the kitchen.

"This looks delicious, Aunt Marie," I told her as we brought the last of the food outside.

"What's wrong with Nikki?" Mimi asked.

"It's just a bad time of the month," I lied. The truth was that I didn't have a clue what was wrong. I wished I knew. Trying to talk to her lately was like trying to talk to a brick wall. The one thing I did know was that Nikki had more bad days than good ones. And I knew she wasn't happy.

Everyone had left. Nikki and David had gone to her mom's and dad's house while I helped Uncle Sid repair some fence. I had always tried to keep my personal business to myself, especially my problems. I figured everyone had their own problems to deal with, and why burden them with mine. But I needed to talk to someone.

"Uncle Sid, can I ask you about something?"

He stopped hammering the nail into the fence post. "Sure you can, John. You know you can ask me about anything."

"It's about women, Uncle Sid. I mean, how do you ever understand them?"

"John, are you talking about women or about one woman in particular?"

I hesitated. "It's Nikki. I don't know what's going on with her. Something is wrong, and she won't talk to me when I try to ask her about it."

Uncle Sid was once again choosing his words carefully. "You know, we've noticed some things lately. Your Aunt Marie worries about you, John. She says she wishes you had more help."

I was surprised. "I didn't realize anyone knew there was a problem."

"You don't get much by Marie. She loves you as if you were her own son, John. You know that. And it really bothers her that your wife doesn't cook. She has come over to clean your apartment a few times while you were in class. She's tried her best to talk Nikki into letting her teach her some simple dishes, but she's not the least bit interested."

"Please tell her not to worry about that, Uncle Sid. With all the food you and Mimi send home with us on Sundays, we make it just fine. I like cereal for breakfast and I am fine with a sandwich for lunch. And Mom did teach me to cook, you know. She didn't want me to ever be dependent on a woman for my meals. If she only knew…"

I thought about how much pleasure it had given my mom to cook a good meal and to have a clean house for 'her boys'. It was just another way she had of showing us how much she loved us.

"Don't get me wrong, Uncle Sid. It would be great to come home to a house that was all picked up and a good home-cooked meal, but I can deal with that not being 'Nikki's thing'. I am a big boy. I can straighten the place up and fix something to eat for David and me. What I am having a hard time with is the fact that Nikki doesn't seem happy. And I don't know what to do to change that."

Uncle Sid listened intently. I continued. "Things seemed fine after David was born. Or maybe I was so busy until I didn't notice there was anything wrong. But I eventually began to notice that she wasn't bonding with him. As soon as I walk in the door, she hands him to me, and it is as if she feels she's off duty or something, that he is my responsibility now that I am at home. She is perfectly content to let me tend to him. Don't get me wrong, Uncle Sid, I don't mind that a bit. I love all the time I spend with David. It's just that I had imagined we would do it together.

"I made an appointment with her doctor and told him how she is acting. He told me that bonding with a baby doesn't always happen immediately for some mothers and for me to be patient. He also said that after the birth of a baby, there are occasional cases when the mother's hormones get out of balance and cause both physical and emotional problems, sometimes serious ones. I was convinced that was the case with Nikki. The doctor told me to bring her in and he would check her out. He found everything to be completely normal. I have since read everything I can get my hands on to try to figure out what could be wrong. I am at a loss, here."

Uncle Sid sat quietly and thought about all I had said. Then he finally spoke. "You know I make it a policy to stay out of the next fellow's business, John. But I hope its okay with you if I say what's on my mind."

"Please do. I am very interested in what you have to say," I told him. It felt good to be able to talk to someone about this.

"Let me ask you something first. Is she taking good care of David?"

"Yes, I don't mean to imply that she isn't. She loves our son. I am sure of that. It's hard to explain. I mean she takes care of his needs. But its like she has this wall up and it keeps her from being close to us.

"I know things aren't like she dreamed of. She wants the best of everything. And she has to do without a lot of things she wants right now. But I keep telling her that our situation is only temporary. Once I get out of college and get a good job, we can have all those things she wants. We are doing fine right now, Uncle Sid. We have everything we could possibly need. But it never seems to be enough for her. When I get home, I am tired and I need to study and sleep. I have very little time for Nikki. And she requires a lot of attention, I can tell you that. She complains because we don't get to go out much. She complains because she can't have an expensive outfit she's seen at the mall. She complains because the place is too small. Maybe it will help now that we will be living in a bigger apartment.

"I feel a lot of guilt, Uncle Sid. She had to give up so much because of me. I wonder sometimes if the problem is that deep down she resents both me and our son and blames us for having to give up the life she had planned on. But I had to give up a lot, too. And I felt a lot of resentment at first, I will admit that. I spent a lot of time feeling sorry for myself...that I didn't get to try out for the football team...that I was working on the weekends when my buddies were going out to the clubs or getting together for a game of poker...that I was up late at night studying when I was so tired I could hardly hold my eyes opened and I just wanted to be in bed asleep...that I was still a teenager and had a wife and baby coming that I had to take care of.

"But at the hospital when David was born, I realized it was all worthwhile. Holding my son for the first time changed everything. I no longer felt sorry for myself or felt any resentment. I felt like the luckiest guy in the world.

"Nikki doesn't feel like that. I can see it in her eyes when she looks at me. And I can't understand why she doesn't see how blessed we are. We were kids in high school and we made a mistake. But we aren't kids in high school anymore. We are married with a child. We are supposed to be partners. We are supposed to be in this together. I am tired of feeling guilty for ruining her life, Uncle Sid. And I tell you something else...one thing I do know is that I don't want to be with someone who doesn't want to be with me."

"Let me ask you another question," Uncle Sid said. "When you look at that boy of yours, do you see a mistake?"

"Heck, no way. When I look at David, I see the best thing that ever happened to me."

"Then put the past in the past, John. You are doing the very best you can to prepare for a good future for you and your family. You can't be responsible for Nikki's actions. You can't control others. I want you to keep something in mind. The 'Colonel' spoiled her rotten. She probably never heard the word 'no' in her entire life until after she got married. She was catered to and made to feel the whole world revolved around her. She needs to grow up and realize that it's not all about her anymore. She needs to learn to put her family first. I feel sorry for her, you know. If she doesn't change the way she looks at things, she will be missing out on all those special family times that she can never get back.

"You hang in there, John. It will all work out."

I thanked Uncle Sid for his time and told him how much it had helped to get it all talked out. I thought about what he said on the way over to pick Nikki and David up. "Things will get better," I thought as we made the drive to our new apartment. "I just have to be patient."

My junior year was the busiest one yet. I made the decision to get my degree in Banking and Finance. The classes required a lot of study time, and I spent hours each night after getting off work doing homework for my Statistics class.

Nikki and David spent a lot of time at her mom's. I knew she liked the fact that between Mimi and Aunt Marie, she had a lot of help with David and she had free time to go to the mall or out to dinner with her friends. I decided to be patient and give her time to adjust to being a wife and a mom. I figured by the time I graduated, I would have more time to give her the attention she wanted, she would be older, and hopefully more ready to 'settle down' to our family life.

In the spring of that year, the Dean of the Business School sent word that he wanted to see me in his office. I had never met him or even been inside the building where the business administration offices were. I left out early the next morning and found my way to his office. He was sitting at his desk looking out the window.

"John David Hughes, Jr., Sir," I said as I shook his hand.

"Sit down, John," he said. "I understand you are a family man."

"Yes, Sir, I have a wife and a son."

"That's nice. And you are here on scholarship?"

"Yes, Sir."

"Well, John, I have some good news for you. Every year the local Banker's Association gives a Banking Scholarship to a student in Banking and Finance in his junior year here at the college. It is based on grade point average, and I am happy to tell you that you have been chosen as this year's recipient. The scholarship is for two thousand dollars. Congratulations!"

I thanked the Dean and walked to my first class. "What a great way to start the day," I thought. With all the scholarship money I had received and the money I was bringing in from the restaurant, it was looking like I would be able to graduate without touching the money my mom and dad had left me for college. "That is going to make a great down-payment on a house for us once I graduate," I thought.

I called Nikki when I got home from class. "Guess what, Nik?" I told her about the banking scholarship.

"That's good." She didn't seem the least bit excited about my news.

I thought about things on the way to work. *What is wrong with this picture? She didn't tell me she was proud of me or even ask what the scholarship was for. She didn't care. It would be nice to come home and have your wife interested in your day. It would be nice to come home and have your wife there, period. Things aren't getting any better.*

I thought back to the day the 'Colonel' had offered to let me off the hook from all my responsibilities. *Maybe it's time to have that talk. Maybe it's time to give her the same option.*

Plans and Decisions

Nikki was sitting up in bed reading when I got home from work that night. "That's great about the scholarship, don't you think?" I asked her.

She didn't look up from her book. "Yea, great."

I went in David's room and watched my son as he peacefully slept. "You are proud of your ole man, right?" I whispered so as not to wake him. He didn't have a care in the world. I wished it could always be that way for him.

I showered and got into bed. "Nikki, we need to talk about something," I said to her.

"Okay," she said as she kept reading.

"Will you please put the book away?"

"What is it?" she asked in frustration as she marked the page and put the book away.

"I need for you to talk to me and tell me what's wrong."

"Oh, that again? I have already told you that nothing is wrong, John."

"Nikki, do you know how frustrating it is when you shut down and won't talk to me?"

"I have nothing to talk to you about," she snapped.

"Fine," I snapped back. "Well, I have plenty to talk to you about, so if you will please hear me out…"

There was that look. Nikki knew how to push my buttons. She could get me upset with just a few words or a glance. I took the time to settle down so my voice would be calm. "You say nothing is wrong, but it is obvious that something is wrong. And you won't talk to me about it. How do you expect me to try to help or make things better when I don't know what I am dealing with? The doctor says you are fine and you say you are fine, so the only thing I can think of is that it has to be me. It is obvious that you aren't happy being married to me. No one is holding a gun to your head and making you stay, you know. If you want out, you need to tell me right now." I stopped talking and waited for her response.

"Where in the world did that come from, John? Surely you don't think I want out of our marriage."

"I don't know what to think anymore, Nikki. Please talk to me."

Instead of talking, Nikki and I made love. I knew it was her way out of continuing our conversation, but it had been a long time since we had been together, and it felt good to be with her again.

The next morning while I was shaving, she came into the bathroom and brought me a cup of coffee. David was still asleep and I was surprised to see her up. "You know, John, I was thinking…what do you think about having another baby?"

I couldn't believe what I was hearing. That's the last thing I would have ever expected to come out of her mouth. My junior year was almost over and I had only one more year to go. The plan was for Aunt Marie and Mimi to keep David so Nikki could go to college and get her degree. "What about college?" I asked her.

"I want David to have a brother or sister, don't you, John?"

"Yes, and I do want to eventually have another child, Nik, but we can wait until after you get your degree."

"John, think about it," she said. "I don't want a big age spread between our children, do you? If we start trying to have a baby right now, there will be about four years between them. And you will be finishing college. The timing seems right."

My wife was full of surprises. Just the night before, I had fully expected her to tell me she wanted out of our marriage. And instead, she was telling me she wanted to have another child. I didn't even think she liked being a mother. I thought about what she said while I showered.

Maybe last night was a wake-up call. Maybe she wants to do it right this time. Maybe she is ready to grow up. Besides,

I want another child. She is right, the timing is perfect. Yes, maybe that is just the thing to do. Let's have another baby.

My senior year had flown by. Graduation was a month away and Nikki was three months pregnant. The phone was ringing as I was headed out the door. "Hello?"

"Is this John Hughes?"

"Yes, it is."

"Mr. Hughes, this is Mrs. Adams at the bank. Mr. Smith has asked that I call and tell you that the job you spoke about is yours. If you will come by sometime today, he would like to talk to you about all the particulars."

I thanked her and said goodbye. I hung up the phone. "I got it, Nik!" I shouted.

The President of the largest bank in the city had wanted to meet the recipient of the Banker's Scholarship. I had gone to his office and met him the week before. We talked a long while and he said he felt I would be an asset to his bank. "What I am thinking about is bringing you into the system as an officer trainee. You would train in each department of the bank for a year, and then at year's end, I would make you a loan officer," he had told me. "Do you think you would be interested?"

I told him I would definitely be interested. He said for me to give him a few days to think about it and he would get back to me. And the call from Mrs. Adams had just made it official...I had the job! I wondered when he would want me to start work. I wondered how much I would be making. I knew it wouldn't be a lot at first, but Mr. Smith had assured me that once I became an officer, I could make a good living there.

I called Rick to tell him that I had gotten the job at the bank. He and Linda were busy getting ready for their June wedding and he asked me to be his best man. He was going to join his father in his real estate firm after graduation. "Congratulations, Man!" he said.

We had a party at the restaurant after graduation. The owner opened up the room in the back for me and my family and friends. The food and drinks were on the house, and he told me how much he was going to miss me around there. I assured him I would be a regular once I was making enough money to afford his food.

"Very funny," he said. "You just make sure you come by to see us every now and then."

It felt good to be finished with college. It felt good to share this time with my family and friends. I looked around the room. Some of the people I had worked with at the restaurant over the past four years were there. Some of my classmates from high school and college were there. Aunt Marie and Uncle Sid were talking to Mimi and the 'Colonel'. They all stopped talking and smiled and clapped as David started dancing to the music playing.

I put my arm around Nikki and pointed at David. "Be sure to get a picture." She smiled and got the camera and walked closer to David and waved at him. He waved back as she took a picture.

I walked over to Rick. "Doesn't it feel good to be out of college?"

"Man, yes," he said. "Now if I can just get this wedding over with."

"What are you boys scheming up now?" Linda came over and put her arms around us.

"We'll never tell," I answered her with a wink and a smile. "I think David has the right idea. Why don't we join him on the dance floor?"

I walked over and picked up my son. "Are you having fun, David?"

"Yes, Dad."

"I love you, Son."

"I love you, too, Dad. I want to dance again."

I thought about my mom and dad and how we used to dance together. I put David down and held his hands and danced with him. This was a time for celebration.

It was October. David's fourth birthday was only a month away. I had been at the bank since July. We had moved from the apartment near campus to a three-bedroom house closer to the 'Colonel's' and Uncle Sid's and only about ten minutes away from the bank. We had decided to rent until we found just the right house to buy. "Hey, we may even decide we want to build, who knows?" I had told Nikki. "Let's keep our options opened for now."

I got a call at the bank. It was the 'Colonel'. "The baby is coming, John. They are on their way to the hospital as we speak."

"Okay, Colonel, I am on my way, too."

I could hear the anxiety in his voice. "Call me as soon as you know something."

There wasn't as much waiting and pacing the floors this time around. Chris was not as stubborn as David had been about making his appearance into the world. My precious little bald-headed baby boy was born early that night. He weighed seven pounds, four ounces.

I called the 'Colonel'. "Everything went well, Sir. He and Nikki are fine. He's a cute one…bald-headed as can be. And Sir, his name is Christopher Walker."

"Thanks for calling, John." I could hear the emotion in the 'Colonel's' voice. "It means a lot to me to have my second grandson share my middle name."

"Yes, Sir, I can't wait for you to see him," I told him.

I called Rick. "I've got another little boy, Rick."

"I am on my way to the hospital," Rick said. "I want to see him."

I was standing at the nursery window watching Chris sleep. I felt a hand on my shoulder. "Where's my cigar, Ole Man?" Rick asked. "And which one of those belongs to you?"

I laughed and pointed Christopher out to him. "He's the one over there."

"I see he's bald like the 'Colonel'," Rick said as he playfully hit me on the arm.

"Hey, watch out!" I laughed again. It was such a relief to have it all over with and for everything to be alright.

"Where's David?"

"He's at Uncle Sid's. You know, I have been worried that he will be jealous. He's been the only little man of the house for awhile now. I've been trying to talk to him and make sure he feels good about the fact he is now going to be a big brother."

"David will be fine," Rick assured me. "Hey, can we go down to the cafeteria and get some coffee? I want to talk to you about something."

"Sure," I said as I looked at Christopher again. "I am ready to get that boy home so I can hold him as much as I like. They have too many rules in these nurseries these days."

Rick and I walked to the cafeteria and got coffee and sat down. "How's the job going?" he asked.

"It's fine as far as jobs go. I guess there is good and bad in every job. But the hours aren't bad and it pays the bills. How do you like the real estate business and working for your dad?"

"That's why I wanted to talk to you, John. I like it a lot. There is money to be made in real estate right now, especially in this area. Let me ask you something…how does it sound to you to be your own boss rather than spend your life working for the 'other fellow'?"

"It sounds good," I answered him.

"Well, I've got a proposition for you."

"Go on, I'm listening."

Rick continued. "You know Dad has built up a nice business."

"Yes, I do." Rick's dad had owned his company for as long as I had known them. He had the reputation of being a good and honest business man and he was well respected in the area.

"Dad says he's got about five to seven more years and then he wants to retire. He is going to teach me the ropes and eventually turn the business over to me. I told him I want you as my partner, John. I told him I wanted us to be in this thing together. He likes you. He thinks it's a great idea. We can learn everything we can from Dad and eventually buy him out and have our own business. It's a win-win. What do you say?"

My head was spinning. "That's a lot to throw at a fellow all at once," I said. "Especially when he's just had a baby."

Rick laughed. "When he's just had a baby is the perfect time to throw this on a fellow. We are talking about our future. We are talking about an opportunity of a lifetime."

I promised Rick I would think about it. "It is quite an offer, for sure."

Nikki and Chris were released from the hospital the following day. I took them home and Mimi followed close behind. I then left for Uncle Sid's to pick up David.

On the way home, I asked him if he'd had a good time.

"Yes, Dad," he said. He told me about getting to ride on the tractor with Uncle Sid and that he had gone down the slide at the school all by himself.

"That's my big boy," I said. "Hey, David, when we get home, the baby will be there." I wondered how his first meeting with his little brother was going to go.

"He's not in Mom's tummy anymore?"

"No, not anymore," I told him. That boy could always put a smile on my face.

When we drove up, David jumped out of the truck and ran inside. Nikki was in bed asleep and Chris was lying in the bassinet in the den. Mimi was getting a bottle ready.

"Let's sit in our chair and feed him," I told David. He loved to sit in the recliner with me at night while I read or watched television. He had gone to sleep many nights sitting in my lap in that chair. David and I sat down and Mimi handed me the baby and the bottle.

David watched closely as Chris started taking the bottle. He looked him over from head to toe. Then he carefully studied my face. "You are his dad, too?" he asked me.

"Yes, Son," I answered. "I am both your dad and Chris' dad."

David continued to watch as I gave Chris his bottle. He leaned down close to him. He took his hand and gently placed it on Chris' head. "Why did you cut off all his hair, Dad?"

I laughed and looked over at Mimi. She looked at me with a huge grin on her face.

"Sometimes babies are born without any hair, David. He will grow some hair soon."

"He's little," he said as he continued to look at him.

"You were that little when you were a baby," I assured him. "And see how big you have grown? Your little brother will grow big, too. But you know what, David? You will always be his big brother. And your little brother will always be glad to have his big brother to look out for him."

"You love him, Dad?" he asked, with those big brown eyes looking up at me.

"Yes, Son, I love him very much," I said as I hugged him. "Just like I love you. I love both my boys very much."

David leaned back over and kissed Chris on the cheek. "Then I love him, too," he said.

Both of the boys were soon asleep. Mimi came and got the baby and took him to his baby bed in his room. I carried David to his room and put him in his bed. I thanked Mimi for all her help and walked her to her car.

I went into the bedroom and lay down beside Nikki. I thought about the offer Rick had made the day before. It had been on my mind since we had talked.

"Is David home?" Nikki was awake.

"I'm sorry; I didn't mean to wake you."

"You didn't," she said.

"How are you feeling?" I asked her. "Do you need anything?"

"I am fine," she assured me.

I told her about David's first meeting with his baby brother. "They are both asleep. Your mom has just gone home."

"Isn't the baby adorable?" she asked.

"Yes, we have two fine boys. I feel like the luckiest guy in the world." I then told her about the offer Rick had made the day before in the hospital.

"What are you going to do?" she asked.

"You know, I told Rick I would think about it, but there's really nothing to think about. There is no way I can turn down such an incredible opportunity. And there is no way I am going to pass on it and spend my life wondering how our lives would have been different if I had taken him up on his offer."

"John, are you sure it's the right thing?"

"Absolutely, one hundred percent sure, Nik."

I kissed her on the forehead. "I am going to check on our boys and fix us something to eat."

I picked up the phone and dialed Rick's number. He answered.

"I just wanted to let you know I am planning to turn in my resignation at the bank in the morning," I told him.

"That's what I wanted to hear," he said.

"I will talk to you tomorrow. Goodbye."

"Goodbye, Partner."

The Growing Years

I changed the station on the radio in my truck as I drove to work that next morning. I was not looking forward to seeing Mr. Smith. I dreaded telling him of my decision. He would have every right to be upset. After all, he had shown a great deal of confidence in me and my potential, and had already invested several months in training me. All I could really do was to go in his office and tell him the truth and hope he understood.

And thankfully, he did understand. He expressed his disappointment that I wasn't staying, but said he couldn't blame me for making the decision I had made. I found out later that he and Mr. Jones, Rick's dad, were old friends and they played golf on occasion. They had even been in a few business ventures together in the past.

"Good luck to you, John," he said as he shook my hand. "Let me know if there is ever anything I can do for you."

I thanked him and told him how much I appreciated the opportunity he had given me.

"We all have to do what's best for us and for our families," he said. "And off the record, I think you are making the right decision."

After I left the bank, I went for a drive. I needed to think. Dad had always said there was nothing more relaxing or no better way to clear a man's head than a good drive down the open road. I turned the music up and headed down the highway.

Things were pretty much the same with Nikki. Just as before, she was perfectly content to lie in bed at night while I got up with the baby. But I didn't mind. It was easier now. I was getting more sleep now that I didn't have to work at night or have the late nights up studying. Besides, those nights with David had been special times for me, and I didn't want to miss out on having those same special times with Chris.

I thought about the female influences in my life. My mom and Aunt Marie were very much alike. They both loved to cook and take care of their homes and pamper their 'boys'. That was their way of showing how much they loved us. But Nikki was different. And that didn't mean she didn't love us. It just meant she didn't enjoy the same things they did.

I thought about my talk with Uncle Sid that day. He said you can't control others. He was right. I no longer questioned whether Nikki wanted to be in the marriage. I had a long talk with myself that day driving down the highway. I realized that I would have to make the decision to accept her just as she was if we were going to be able to make our marriage work.

You can't control others, and you can't change them. Everyone is different. And maybe I have been unfairly comparing Nikki to my mom and to Aunt Marie. No, I can't change my wife, but I can change my attitude toward her and how I react to her. She is the mother of my children, and I will accept her just the way she is. I will love her and do the best I can to provide for her and for the boys. I will do my part to always be there for them and to make sure they grow up in a healthy environment and a happy home.

"How are the boys doing?" Linda asked.

Rick and I were at the office late that afternoon studying for our real estate exam. We had completed all of our pre-licensing courses and were scheduled to take the exam on the following Friday.

"Let's just say I had better take my vitamins," I said. "That Chris keeps me hopping. And poor David is running himself nuts trying to keep him in line. The little fellow is very serious about his role as big brother. He worried himself silly over Chris' bald head until his blonde hair finally started to come in. And now that he's walking, the little guy's curious nature is constantly keeping him in trouble. David spends his time following him around and telling him he needs to mind."

Linda and Rick laughed and I continued, "With David, the word 'no' always meant 'no'. The word 'no' is nothing more than a challenge to Chris. The boy is into everything."

Linda was working as a counselor at the high school and had come in after work to clean our office building.

Rick looked up from his book. "Hey, why don't we all go out to dinner Friday night after the exam?"

"That sounds like a plan," I said.

Linda hesitated. "Do you think 'Her Highness' can break away from her busy schedule long enough to go out to dinner?"

"Be nice," Rick said.

Linda had very little patience with Nikki these days. When Rick had told her that he and John were going to be business partners, she had tried to make a special effort to become better friends with her. "You just can't get close to that girl," she had told Rick in frustration. "She is just as arrogant and selfish as she was when we were all in high school."

She had promised Rick she would do her best to be tolerant of Nikki for John's sake, but she wasn't doing a good very job of it today. She didn't mind pitching in around the office, but she had worked all day and was tired and was not happy with the fact that Nikki had never once lifted a finger to help out.

"What does she do all day, anyway? She doesn't work. She doesn't do anything around the house. Aunt Marie and Mrs. Jackson take care of the boys while you are at work."

"That's a very good question," I answered her. "I don't have a clue what she does all day. After Chris was born, I talked to her about going back to school or even getting a job. Since she doesn't seem to enjoy the domestic life, I thought it would be good for her to have something to occupy her time outside the home. But she doesn't seem to be interested."

"Well, I'm not surprised about that. That is typical Nikki. How in the world do you put up with her, John? Rick wouldn't put up with me for two minutes if I acted like that. Right, Rick?" she asked looking over at him.

Rick threw his hands in the air. "Hey, you two leave me out of this. So, are we going out to dinner on Friday night or not?" Rick wanted to change the subject.

He understood Linda's frustrations, but John was a very private man, and for the most part, kept things to himself. Over the years, Rick had learned to give him space, and when he was ready to talk, he would. He felt they should keep their opinions to themselves unless he asked for them. He gave Linda a look.

"Don't pay any attention to her, John. You know Linda sometimes gets carried away. She doesn't mean anything by it."

Linda realized she had probably said too much. "Yea, I'm sorry, John. I didn't mean anything by it. I hope I didn't say anything that offended you. It's just that I love you and I get so frustrated with her...I just want to shake some sense into that girl at times."

I assured her I was not offended. "Hey, we've all known each other for a long time. I'm glad I have you guys to talk to, and you can always say what's on your mind, especially when it's true."

We all laughed and I gathered my books. "Speaking of which... I had better head home. I promised David we would go out for hamburgers tonight."

I was sitting in my recliner later that night going over my study notes once again when Nikki walked through.

"What are you doing?" she casually asked.

"I'm studying for my test," I answered.

"Test?" she asked as she kept walking.

"Yes, you do remember that Rick and I are taking our Real Estate License Exam on Friday, don't you?"

"Yes, I remember," she said.

"I'm a little nervous about it. It's been awhile since I've taken a big test." I waited for a response and there was none. Her disinterest unnerved me. I continued. "Rick said we should all go out to eat when we are finished taking the exam."

She stopped and turned to face me. "You mean with Rick and Linda?"

"Yes, of course that's what I mean."

"I don't think so," she said in almost a whisper.

I looked at her in disbelief. "What do you mean you don't think so?" I asked. "All you have done lately is to complain that you never get to go out, and now that you have the opportunity, you say you don't want to. That makes a lot of sense."

"I do want to go out, but why with Rick and Linda?" she asked.

"To celebrate, Nikki...well, hopefully to celebrate. This exam is really important to our careers, you know. And to share this time with our friends."

"They aren't my friends, John," she said. "They are your friends."

I could feel my patience wearing thin. "What are you talking about? Rick is the best friend any guy could have. And Linda is, too. Rick and I are going to be business partners and we will all be spending a lot of time together. It wouldn't hurt you to try harder, you know. Linda was just asking about the boys today."

"And just where did you see Linda?" she asked, obviously aggravated.

I hated how she crossed her arms and rolled her eyes at the mention of Linda's name. "She was at the office today," I managed to calmly answer. "She came in to clean the place up a bit. And while we are on the subject, do you know how embarrassing it is when Linda has worked all day and comes in afterwards to help us out and you never even bother to show?"

"I am not a maid, John," she said quickly.

"Yes, that is obvious," I said sarcastically as I looked around our messy den. "Look, Nikki, it's not about being a maid. It's about everyone trying to pitch in and help out right now."

"Well, I don't care to go out with Linda," she said. "Linda doesn't have anything to say that I want to hear."

"Stop being such a snob, Nikki. If you give her a chance, you just might see that you are wrong about that. And besides," I continued, now visibly upset, "you just might learn a thing or two about being supportive of your husband."

"Oh, that's a nice thing to say, John."

"The truth can hurt sometimes, can't it?" I asked getting out of my chair.

"Well, isn't it too bad that you aren't married to Miss Perfect Linda?" she yelled with her hand on her hip.

"Now, that's real mature," I said. "And will you lower your voice? You will wake the boys."

She stormed out of the room and I followed her. I spoke, now with anger in my voice. "Okay, so maybe you don't care about my career, but you have a horse in the race, too, you know. If I do well, then you do well. Have you ever thought of that? Or have you been too busy shopping with 'Daddy's' credit card that you haven't had time to think of things like that?

"Yes, I know about the credit cards," I continued as she looked at me surprised.

"Well, at least Daddy cares that I have nice clothes," she screamed at me defensively.

"Oh poor Nikki...so deprived! Thank goodness you have Daddy to take care of you," I said disgusted. "Fine, you stay home with the boys Friday night and I will go out to celebrate with Rick and Linda."

"I'm not staying home Friday night. I'll go out with MY friends."

"So, what else is new?" I yelled.

"Whatever!" she screamed as she walked away from me.

I went outside and paced back and forth on the deck until I calmed down. I then went to check on my boys. They were sound asleep.

Rick and I were on our way to the bank. Mr. Smith had called and had the loan papers ready to be signed. "Where does the time go?" I asked.

"Time flies when you're having fun, Buddy," Rick said. "Can you believe it? Today dad's real estate firm will be ours."

The decision to become Rick's partner in the real estate business had been one of the best decisions I had ever made. We learned everything we could from his dad and got the training and experience we needed to keep the business successful. We had both gotten our real estate broker licenses and even though those early years had been lean, we were now making a good living.

"You are right, Rick. It makes all the difference when you enjoy what you do."

"Oh, by the way, after we get these papers signed, I have something I want you to see," he said.

"Congratulations!" Mr. Smith said as he shook our hands. "It's always good to see you, John. And Rick, be sure to tell your dad to get in touch with me. He will have time now for some golf."

"I will do that," Rick said. We thanked him for the loan.

"Thank you. And let me know if there's anything else we can do here at the bank for you."

"Okay, Partner, it's official. What do you want me to see?"

"I had rather show you," Rick said as he drove out of the city. "By the way, how is the house hunting going?"

"You know, I haven't found anything yet. I am thinking about buying some land and just building what I want. I have been looking at some house plans."

We were about twenty minutes south of the city. "Man, the countryside is beautiful here," I said. "I've never been in this area before."

Rick slowed down and turned. He went through a gate that was standing open with two brick columns on each side. He stopped the car and pointed to the top of the hill. "I wanted you to see this house, John."

I looked up and saw a two-story brick home sitting on top of the hill. "Very nice," I said. "What is it...about four thousand square feet? And look at that big porch running all the way around the front and the sides." There was a big swing and two huge, wooden rocking chairs sitting on the front.

"I know. It's real nice and it's about to go on the market. I told the guy who owns it that I wanted you to see it before it is listed. I have the key. Let's go check it out."

We drove up the hill and got out and walked around the back of the house and through a three-car garage. The door opened into a big kitchen. There was a dining room and spacious den and family room. One end of the house had two bedrooms and a bath that would be perfect for the boys. There was a large master bedroom and bathroom on the other end. There was another bedroom and bath on the second floor, along with a huge space that could be used for a study and another bedroom and storage. There was plenty of closet space, a utility room, a huge deck out back and twenty acres of land.

"This is perfect. And I love the location."

"I thought you would want to see it. The owner is coming to the office in the morning. You two can talk then."

I got the key from Rick and took Nikki and the boys to the house later that afternoon. "Well, what do you think?" I asked her as we walked through.

"I love it, John! Can we afford to buy this place?"

"I love it, too. And yes, I think we can. I am supposed to meet with the owner in the morning, and I will know more then."

The boys were happily running out back. "What do you think, boys? Would you like to live here?"

"Can we get a dog, Dad?" David asked.

"Yes, I think we can get a dog."

David got down on his hands and knees and started barking. Chris jumped on his back.

I laughed and look at Nikki. "I think that's a yes."

"It's been crazy, Uncle Sid. How many people do you know who close on a business and a house the same week? So, what do you think about the place?"

"This is quite a find, John." Uncle Sid looked out back. "This is a great place to raise the boys. Congratulations on both the business and the house. Sounds like you got quite a deal."

"I did. I lucked up on this place, for sure. The guy built the house and got transferred before he ever got a chance to move in. He was in a hurry to sell and thanks to Rick, this all fell into place at exactly the right time."

"Oh by the way, John, that family reunion in Georgia I've been telling you about is coming up soon. I hope you will try to go. Your mama's folks all want to see you and meet Nikki and the boys."

The next few weeks were hectic as we got the new place ready to move into. Nikki was excited about having a new house and stayed busy buying furniture and decorating each room. She was in good spirits and it was great to finally have everything done so we could move in.

I grilled hamburgers and hotdogs and we sat at the kitchen table and ate our first meal in our new home.

"How would you guys like to take an airplane ride?" I asked them.

The boys got out of their chairs and began to jump up and down. "Really, Dad, we can ride in an airplane?"

"Yes, I want to go to Georgia to the family reunion." I looked at Nikki. "We've never really been on a real vacation. What do you say, Nik?"

The reunion was held in the fellowship hall of the church my mom and Uncle Sid had grown up in. All of my aunts and uncles and about thirty cousins were there. I hadn't seen mom's brothers and sisters, except for Uncle Sid, of course, since mom's funeral. Everyone brought food and there was enough there to feed an army.

"Aunt Sue, this is the best chicken I have had in a long, long time. It tastes just like my mom's."

Aunt Sue smiled. "Well, we learned from the same mama, you know. I am so glad you came and brought your family, John. You have grown into such a fine young man. Your mama would be so proud."

It felt good to be with mom's family and I felt her close to me. They brought pictures of her when she was younger that I had never seen before. They talked of their childhoods and what it was like to grow up in such a large family back in those days.

Uncle Sid drove us to the old home place where they grew up. "It hasn't changed much around here," he said. "I can still see Grandma rocking away in that old rocking chair that sat out on the front porch."

After the reunion, I rented a car and drove to the east coast. The boys saw the ocean for the first time. I sat on the sandy beach and watched Nikki building sandcastles with them. They filled their little buckets and worked hard dumping them until they had her legs completely buried in the sand. They laughed and ran in circles around her and fell into her arms. That was the Nikki I had fallen in love with so many years ago…the happy, carefree, girl with the beautiful smile on her face. I missed her. I wished the boys could have that Nikki with them all the time.

That night we all piled up in a king-sized bed in the hotel room and ordered room service and watched a movie. The movie ended and the boys were sound asleep. They both had smiles on their faces.

Chris walked over to the window of his dad's hospital room. He looked down at the parking lot. "Where is Dr. Lewis? He should be here by now."

Restless

Chris made another trip to the window. He walked to the door and looked down the hall. "I will be right back, Dad." He walked down to the nurses' station.

"Have you seen Dr. Lewis?" he asked the nurses.

One of the nurses answered him. "He's running late today, Chris. He had an emergency surgery this afternoon. We expect him soon. Is there anything we can help you with?"

He looked around for Nurse Fulton, but it wasn't time for her shift. "No thanks, will you please tell Dr. Lewis I need to speak to him as soon as he gets here?"

Chris walked back down the hall to his dad's room. He walked over once again to the window and looked down at the cars and people below.

Something was different today. Early on, they had been told about reflex actions and involuntary movements. "They are common in comatose patients," Dr. Liebovich had warned them. "Many times the families mistake them for signs that the patient is responding and it gives them a false sense of hope. We want you to know what to expect."

Chris had spent many hours sitting by his father's bed and closely observing him. He was all too familiar with the jerks and twitches of his body as he continued to lay there oblivious to his surroundings.

He knew not to make anything of them. But this was something different.

"I hear you have been looking for me, Chris." He turned around to see Dr. Lewis standing by his dad's bed. He was looking at his chart.

"Yes. Something is different with Dad today. I don't know how to explain it and there's not one thing in particular I can put my finger on. It's just this sense I have. Dad seems restless to me."

Dr. Lewis looked back down at the chart in his hands. "How are we doing today, Mr. Hughes?" He pushed his eyelids up and looked into his eyes with a light. He listened to his heart. "His blood pressure is up a bit."

"What does this mean, Dr. Lewis?"

"I'm not sure, Chris. We'll keep a close eye on him."

Three weeks had passed since the accident. Chris knew the more time that went by, the less chance the doctors were giving him of coming out of this. He knew they had hoped for some improvement by now.

Dr. Lewis left to see his other patients and Chris rubbed his dad's feet and legs. He had been lying on his back for awhile. He called for an orderly to help get him turned onto his side. They said it was important to keep his positions changed and his body weight distributed on different areas to avoid pressure soars. He and the orderly got him turned on his right side.

"There, Dad, is that better?" Chris asked as he propped some pillows against his back. "David will be here soon."

It had always taken a lot of energy to keep Nikki happy. I realized driving home from work that late summer afternoon that I was emotionally spent. She had been happy for awhile when we first bought the new house. But as with everything else, the newness had soon worn off and the happiness had been short-lived. The wide mood swings were starting again and getting worse each day.

It was important to me to know where I stood with people. I wanted them to either always speak to me or never speak to me. If they liked me, fine, and if they didn't, fine, just as long as they were consistent and I knew what to expect.

How ironic that I didn't know where I stood with the one person who I was supposed to know better than anyone else. I didn't know which Nikki to expect each day when I got home.

I remembered how I felt the morning I woke up after ten years of marriage and realized I was looking into the eyes of a stranger. I didn't understand how you could spend your entire adult life with someone and not know them.

I didn't look forward to going home. If not for the boys, I would just keep on driving. I had been riding this emotional roller coaster with my wife for way too long and I was exhausted.

I was not only exhausted, I was also angry. This should have been a good time for our family. We should have been enjoying all those things I had worked so hard for.

I had seen a man on television talking about relationships. He said that the quality of a relationship is measured by how well it meets the needs of both parties. That really struck a nerve. I couldn't remember the last time my wife was interested in meeting any of my needs. I couldn't even remember the last time it felt like she cared.

I felt this huge, empty space between us. I was in a marriage and yet I felt so alone.

I pulled into the garage and David ran out to meet me. Chris was close behind.

"How was the first day of school, Guys?" I asked as I grabbed one in each arm. David had just started the sixth grade and thankfully, Christopher had made it out of the first and into the second. He had told me more than once that he had other things he wanted to do rather than go to school.

"School is always fun the first day," David said. "Dad, it's a great day for a road trip."

I knew exactly what that statement meant. The little guy had been quite sensitive to his mom's moods for a long time now, and quite perceptive in how I dealt with them. From the time the boys were very small, I had made it a practice to load them up and head out for a drive when Nikki was having a particularly bad day. David had caught on at a very early age.

I went inside. Nikki was lying on the couch. She didn't get up or speak. I looked at my watch.

"What have you guys been doing since you got home from school?" I asked.

"I'll show you, Dad," David said as I followed him into his room.

He went over to the activity table and proudly showed me the picture he had painted.

"That's a great picture, Son. And is your homework all done?"

"Yes, Sir," he answered.

I looked at Chris. "And what have you been up to, Christopher?"

"Just playing, Dad," he said.

"And is your homework done?"

Chris looked down and shook his head. "Not yet."

"Okay, Son, we'll get it done later. Let's go for that drive and then go somewhere to eat. Where do you want to go?"

"The Italian place," Chris answered quickly.

"The Italian place? You've never wanted to eat at the Italian place before, Chris."

"Mom likes Italian food," he said as he ran into the den. "Maybe if we go there, she will want to come with us.

"Mom, we are going out to eat Italian food. Do you want to come?"

Nikki sat up on the couch and picked up the magazine that was lying on the floor. "Not today," she answered him.

David walked over to the couch and patted his mom on the back. "We will bring you something to eat, Mom."

It broke my heart to see the disappointment on Chris's face as he turned around and walked outside. We got in the truck. "I'll be right back," I told the boys.

Nikki was still sitting on the couch when I went back inside. "What in the world is your problem?" I asked.

"I don't have a problem," she said, obviously aggravated by the question. "I don't know of any law that says I can't stay home while you go out to eat."

"Well, there should be." I could feel the anger building inside me. "Didn't you see the disappointment on Chris's face? Don't you realize how much a little boy craves his mother's attentions? Don't you notice how happy it makes them when we all go out and do things together as a family?"

I continued. "They've been in school. You've had all day to sit your butt on the couch and read your magazines. I will never understand you." I turned around and walked back outside.

I did suspect that this latest episode had absolutely nothing to do with the boys and everything to do with me. They just happened to get caught in the crossfire, and there was nothing alright about that. They didn't understand. They felt rejected and they were hurting.

Yes, this was all about getting back at me. She was making a statement. I had changed the rules late in the game and she was not happy about that at all.

Uncle Sid had tried to talk to me early on about the pattern that was developing with Nikki in our marriage. He had tried to tell me how important it was to communicate and to set the ground rules. He said if you didn't want to put up with something for the rest of your life, then you had better get it settled from the start.

He told me about an incident that happened the first year he and Aunt Marie were married. "I went out one Friday night to play cards with the guys," he said. "Marie was fine with that. Well, we got into the 'juice' that night and I wasn't even thinking about the time or the fact that it was late and I should at least be respectful enough to call. I got home late that night, or I should say, early that next morning, and Marie was still sitting up… waiting and worrying. She got up out of that chair, came over to me, and put her finger right in my face. She told me that she wouldn't live like that and it had better never happen again. I knew she meant it, and it never did happen again. She set the ground rules, John. And there are some things going on in your marriage that you had better change now, or you will be sorry later on."

I had known what Uncle Sid was saying to me, and I wished I had listened to him way back then, but I didn't. I had been guilty of picking right up where the 'Colonel' had left off and letting Nikki get away with doing whatever she pleased.

After reading everything I could get my hands on, I had finally come across an article that could have been written specifically about Nikki. It talked about the possible consequences of failing to set boundaries for our children and 'spoiling them'. It said that many of these children grow up to feel a sense of entitlement…that an overindulged child can many times grow up to be a self-centered, unmotivated and depressed adult lacking empathy for others. That definitely described my wife.

I was sick and tired of coming home from work each day and having to enter the 'it's all about Nikki and her needs zone'. She expected the world to stop turning and for everything to revolve around her, and I had been doing nothing but feeding those expectations for all these years.

Lately, I had started giving her the same 'I don't care about what you need' attitude that she had been giving me. I had started ignoring her. Nikki did not like getting a taste of her own medicine. She was not getting her way and the little girl inside her was sitting on the couch pouting.

"She's never going to grow up," I said to myself as I got back into the truck and drove down the road. I wanted to get the boys' minds off the situation at home. I started singing with the radio and David joined in.

"I don't want to go to the Italian place anymore." Chris was sitting on the backseat. I could see his sad little face in the rear-view mirror. His bottom lip was quivering as he fought back the tears.

I turned the radio down. "That's fine, Son. We can go wherever you like."

"Dad, why doesn't Mom want to go with us? Is it because I am bad?" he asked.

David was sitting on the front seat halfway between me and the door. He had stopped singing and was turned facing me as he waited for my answers to his brother's questions.

I turned onto a little dirt road I saw ahead and drove into an open field and stopped the truck. I had always tried to shoot straight with my boys, but found myself making more and more excuses for Nikki these days. They were getting older and were seeing my answers for just what they were…excuses. I was fast running out of explanations for their mother's behavior. I wanted to be as honest with them as I could.

I turned around to face Chris. "I want you boys to listen to me real close, okay?" They both nodded their heads and said that they would.

"There are days like today when your mom doesn't feel so good inside and she needs to be alone. And it has absolutely nothing to do with you being bad. It isn't your fault and you have done nothing wrong. Your mom loves you very much and she loves being with you. We just need to be patient when she doesn't feel good and is trying to feel better. Do you understand what I am saying?"

"Is Mom sick?" David asked.

"No, Son, she's not sick. But sometimes she gets unhappy when things don't go as she planned, and it makes her feel bad. Do you remember when you had the flu last year? You just wanted to lie in bed and you didn't feel like going to school or playing or eating. You just wanted to be alone until you felt well again."

"Yes, I remember," David answered.

"Well, it's a little like that with your mom. Her body isn't sick like yours was, but her mind feels sad at times and she wants to be alone until she feels happy again."

The explanation seemed to satisfy David. I looked back at Chris. He wasn't as upset as he had been earlier. "Look guys," I said as I pointed back over the mountains in the distance behind us. "Look at that beautiful sunset."

We got out. I let the tailgate down and we sat on the back of the truck and looked at the awesome colors in the sky. "My dad taught me to appreciate the beauty of a sunset," I told them. "He said whenever he saw a sunset, he would take the time to stop and take a deep breath and relax; that no matter what he was going through in his life, a sunset always reminded him that God was in control and that everything was going to be alright."

I took a deep breath and looked up at the heavens. I felt a sense of peace. I looked at my boys. They were looking out at the Montana sky, both immersed in their own thoughts.

My instinct had always been to protect them from everything bad that ever happened. But today I held back. A father's job is not only to protect his children, but also to prepare them for a world that can be quite tough at times. They were growing up and I would not always be there to fight their battles for them.

I thought about my dad. He had not only protected me, he had also prepared me for a world that I would someday have to face alone. He loved me and nurtured me and was always there for me. But he always seemed to know when the time was right to step aside and let me take some knocks and even some falls. And when those falls came, he taught me how to get back up and dust myself off and start all over again.

He loved me enough to prepare me to face a tough world. He knew he would not always be there to help me face it. I didn't realize until this very moment how hard that is for a father to do. It is much easier to protect our children than to prepare them.

I looked at my precious sons. They were still my baby boys and there would be a lot more protecting for a long time yet, but today was a time for me to step aside and give them the opportunity to deal with their emotions in their own way. It was a time for them to figure out a way to find their own sense of peace.

We sat in the back of the truck late that afternoon until the sun had completely disappeared over the mountains.

"Let's go eat...I am starving," Chris said.

"Me, too," David said.

"Me, three," I said as we climbed back into the truck and headed down the road.

The Separation

David had come to relieve Chris and to spend the weekend at the hospital. Chris had told him about his conversation earlier with Dr. Lewis. They had sat by their father's bed, one on each side, for a couple of hours watching him.

"I see exactly what you mean, Chris. It's like Dad is agitated."

"Yes, that's exactly the right word…agitated. I told Dr. Lewis that Dad seems restless to me."

They got up and walked to the far side of the room. "Dr. Lewis said he didn't know what that could mean. His blood pressure is up a bit today."

"Go home and get some rest, Chris. I'll call you if I notice any other changes."

David watched as Chris paced back and forth near the door. He could tell something was on his mind. "Talk to me, Little Brother. Dad is not the only one who is restless today. What's going on with you?"

Chris stopped pacing and looked over at his dad. He walked closer to David. "I've been thinking about Mom."

"Let's sit and talk, Chris." David sat down in the recliner by the door and motioned for Chris to sit in the chair next to him.

"What have you been thinking about Mom?" he asked.

"I miss her, David, you know I do. But I have been thinking about how things were when we were younger, and I have so many questions.

I wonder what was going on with her back then, and what happened to cause such a change after Charlie was born.

"You know, everyone thought I was just jealous of Charlie since I had been the youngest for so long. But the truth was that I despised my little brother when he was little. I saw him getting all of the love and affection that I had so wanted when I was his age, and I didn't understand what he had done so right and what I had done so wrong.

"Eventually I realized Mom wasn't just reaching out to Charlie, but to all of us. She had a talk with me one day and apologized to me for not being the Mom she should have been. She told me she loved me. David, that was the first time I had ever heard her say those words to me, and I was twelve years old. I didn't even know how to act.

"Do you know what happened, David? You were older than I was. Do you know what caused Mom to change after Charlie was born?"

David listened to Chris and sat quietly as he thought about what he had said. He very well remembered those early years, and even though he was older, he had felt many of those same things that Chris had. Mom had come to him, too, and had apologized and told him she loved him.

"You know, Chris, Dad and I had a long talk about things back when I was still living at home. I had come across their marriage license one day and had figured out they had to get married when they were so young because Mom was pregnant with me."

"I didn't know that, David." Chris was surprised to hear that his mom had gotten pregnant before she was married.

"Yes," David continued, "and I had gone through a lot of guilt because I felt like any time there were problems in our family, it was somehow my fault. I told Dad that because of me, his options had been taken away from him when he was still just a teenager, and I was sorry.

"You know what he told me? He told me that I was never to feel guilty again…that it surely hadn't been my fault. He said that he and Mom had made a mistake and had to start their family sooner than they had planned because of it, but he had no regrets; that you and I were the best things that had ever happened to him and he didn't even want to think of his life without us in it.

"And he said a man always has options…that he had options and he chose his boys. I tell you, Chris, that man lying over there in that bed was always there for us, and no matter what was going on with Mom, he always held it together for us.

"We talked about Mom that day. I asked him pretty much what you have just asked me now. He told me about a talk he had with Uncle Sid one day and how Uncle Sid had said that Grandpa had pretty much spoiled Mom and because of that, it took her awhile to grow up.

"For whatever reason, Dad put up with it for all those years. He said he couldn't help but to love the mother of his children, but I think more than anything else, he did it all for us."

David then smiled. "Chris, I love Jessica with all my heart. But I promise you, I could never put up with what Dad did."

Chris was smiling now, too. "Did you know the first thing I asked Paige after we started dating was if she could cook?"

David laughed and leaned back in his chair and continued. "Chris, do you remember when Mom and Dad separated?"

"Of course I remember."

"I really do believe that when Dad finally left Mom, and she realized he was serious and she was going to lose him, it scared her to death. I believe the only reason he ever came back to her was because of Charlie. And that would explain why she changed after he was born. She wasn't the best at showing it, Little Brother, but she truly did love you and me and Dad. And we just need to be thankful for those good years we had with her before the accident."

"And I am thankful, David." Chris walked over to his dad's hospital bed. "I am going home for awhile, Dad. I hope you have a good weekend. I love you."

The next couple of years of our marriage could best be described as two people 'going through the motions'. We had celebrated Chris' eleventh birthday and David had just turned fifteen. They were busy with their school activities and their friends and Rick and I were putting in a lot of time at the office.

Nikki and I were living more like roommates than as husband and wife. Our latest battle was over our finances and her incessant shopping. Rick and I were making good money with our real estate business, but Nikki was spending it faster than I could bring it home.

I sat down and fixed a budget. My goal was to pay the house off early and to get the boys' college funds in good shape. We had enough money coming in to do that and to still have plenty left over for savings and to live comfortably.

"Work with me here, Nikki." We sat down and I explained the budget figures and how easily my plan could be accomplished if we would just be smart with our spending.

The next morning I had gotten out of the shower and was in the closet getting something to wear for work. I tripped over a sack that was in the closet floor. I looked inside and saw four very expensive outfits that she had just purchased the day before.

I went over to the bed and dumped the contents of the sack out beside her where she lay. "I see you failed to tell me about this latest shopping spree when we talked about our finances last night."

She rolled over. She wasn't the least bit concerned with what I had to say.

"Well, you can take it all back today. Maybe that will get your attention."

She sat up in bed and looked at me. "I'm not taking that back."

"Nikki, do you know how long and hard I have to work to pay for these clothes? I want you to get up and come with me to the closet."

"Leave me alone, John," she said.

I walked to the closet and stood there waiting for her. She finally got up and came to the closet door. Our large, walk-in closet was overstuffed with her clothes and shoes just as her closet had been all those years ago in her bedroom when she was a teenager. But the closet was much bigger now. There were outfits hanging that still had the tags on them.

"Do you see this waste?" I asked her. "This has to stop. I want those clothes on the bed taken back today." I got dressed and went to the kitchen.

The boys were sitting at the kitchen table eating cereal. David was reading the back of the cereal box and Chris was propped up on the table trying to keep his eyes open. "Are you about ready to go to school?" I asked as I poured a cup of coffee.

Nikki came into the kitchen and I handed her the coffee I had just poured and grabbed another cup.

I was not expecting what happened next. I turned around and started walking to the kitchen table to sit down. All of a sudden, the cup of hot coffee came flying at me. The cup fell to the floor and broke and the coffee splattered all over my face and hands and clothes.

"I hate you!" she screamed.

I quickly went to the sink and started rinsing my face and hands with cold water. I took my shirt and pants off as the coffee started soaking through my clothes and began to burn my skin.

I looked over at David and Chris. They sat motionless, a look of disbelief on their faces. "You boys go on and get in the car," I told them. "I will be out in just a minute to take you to school."

They didn't say a word. They got up from the table and went to the car as I had asked them to do. I knew they were as shocked about what had just happened as I was. It had happened so fast, and I couldn't believe what she had just done. This was over the top, even for Nikki.

I went to the bedroom. I got some more clothes out of the closet. Nikki was sitting on the edge of the bed. She got up and came over to me. "I am so sorry," she said. "I don't know why I did that. I love you, John." She reached out to hug me.

They say every man has his breaking point, and this particular morning, I had mine. My dad's words were playing in my head. "Never speak words in anger, John. You can never take them back. Bite your tongue or remove yourself from a situation until you cool off."

I have always tried to do just that, Dad. But I'm sorry... today I say what needs to be said.

I grabbed my wife's hands and removed them from my shoulders and slowly walked her over to the bed. She sat down and looked up at me and said the words again. "I love you, John."

I took a deep breath and began to speak. "Those are just words, Nikki. I haven't felt your love for a long time."

I paused and took another deep breath and continued. "You know, Nikki, I have put up with your crap for years. I have worried that something was physically or mentally wrong with you. After all, the Nikki I knew and loved wouldn't be acting like this. But after hearing all those doctors through the years say you are just fine, I can only assume one thing…that you resent me and feel like I ruined your life and you have made it your mission to punish me and make me miserable.

"Look, I am sorry you had to marry so young and be a mother so young and give up those things you had dreamed of doing. But you keep forgetting that I had to do the same. And you know what? I can't imagine a life without those boys, and I have no regrets. I just wish for your sake and for their sakes that you could feel the same.

"I know you are unhappy, and I will tell you right now that it's your own fault. You are selfish and spoiled and even after all these years, you haven't grown up. And it's sad, Nikki, because you are so caught up in your own wants and needs that you can't see how blessed you are. You have two fine, healthy boys who love you so much, and who would do anything in this world for you. You have a life that most women can only dream of, and you don't have a clue how to be thankful or how to appreciate any of it.

"I'm tired, Nikki. I'm tired of pretending that everything is alright. I'm tired of being with someone who doesn't want to be with me. I'm tired of not feeling appreciated. I'm tired of trying to make you happy. I'm tired of making excuses for you and your actions. And most of all, I'm tired of believing that things are going to get better when we both know that they aren't."

I stopped for a minute to gather my thoughts. I walked across the bedroom and back to her. I looked at her face. She sat there as motionless and as speechless as the boys had been earlier at the kitchen table. I finally had her attention, I had more to say, and I was going to say it.

"I have always shown you respect and insisted that the boys do the same, even when you didn't necessarily deserve it. And then you go and pull the stunt you pulled this morning? In front of our boys, Nikki! Let me tell you one thing. You can think what you want about me and you can say what you want about me, but don't you ever disrespect me again like that in front of my sons."

I went into the bathroom and splashed more cold water on my face and combed my hair again and put on my clothes. I walked back to her once again. She still sat in the same position on the edge of the bed.

"Look, it is obvious that I have failed you miserably. I have never been able to live up to your expectations. Yes, I admit it, Nikki. I am a failure. I have not been the man you needed me to be. I have not been the husband that you deserved. I am done...finished...I GIVE!"

I walked out of the bedroom and slammed the door behind me. I walked to the car. I drove down the driveway. "We'll go pick you up some breakfast," I said.

"We were finished," David quietly answered.

I headed toward the school.

"Does Mom really hate you, Dad?" Chris asked.

"Your mom doesn't hate anyone, Chris. It's just that she's very unhappy with herself right now, and when we aren't happy with ourselves, we sometimes tend to lash out at those closest to us."

We pulled up to the school. "Listen, how about I pick you up after school and we go hang out at the mall for awhile and then get some pizza."

"Okay, Dad," David said as he got out of the car.

"Have a good day at school. And don't worry, Guys, everything is going to be alright."

I was at work before Rick that morning. I was anxious for him to get there. I needed to talk. As soon as he walked in the door, I began telling him about the morning's events.

"She threw a hot cup of coffee on me, Rick, and she told me she hated me right there in front of the boys. Can you believe that?"

Rick sat down. He shook his head. "Linda and I have talked about it many times. She won't be surprised that this has happened. She has always said that you have more patience than any man she has ever known, but that one day Nikki is going to really mess up and then even you will have had enough."

"Well, she was right. I have definitely had enough. I guess I have finally lost all hope that things will get better. They are getting worse instead of better. And we aren't doing the boys any favors by continuing to stay together and put them through this."

I stood there still in disbelief. "I mean, come on, when your wife says she hates you and throws a hot cup of coffee on you, then I think she might be trying to tell you something."

Rick looked over at his longtime friend. It was just like John to somehow manage to find some humor in even the worst of situations.

"What can I do to help?" he asked.

"I need some time away from Nikki. I need some time to clear my head and figure out what to do. Would it be alright if I stay at your house for a couple of days until I find a place?"

"Sure, John, you know you are welcome to stay as long as you like," Rick said.

"Linda won't mind?" I asked.

Rick grinned. "Are you kidding? Linda loves you more than she loves me."

I managed a smile and thanked Rick. I tried to stay busy at work. I wanted to get my mind off things for awhile.

I picked the boys up at school that afternoon. We went to the mall and then to eat pizza. I needed to talk to them and I needed to be as honest as I could possibly be.

I studied their faces. I could see that they were worried and upset. "You boys are growing up so fast. I love you both so much." I was fighting back the tears. "Listen, Guys, I am going to stay at Rick's for awhile."

Chris finished his last bite of pizza and asked the question that had been on his mind. "Dad, are you and Mom going to get a divorce?"

David sat quietly. He hadn't eaten any of his pizza. They both deserved an honest answer. But the truth was that I didn't know.

"I don't know what is going to happen, Chris. But no one is talking about a divorce. Your mom and I are having some problems, and the best thing right now is for us to have some time apart to think about things and to decide what is best for our family."

I assured them that we would still be spending a lot of time together just as we always had. I would still take them to school and see them each afternoon and we would spend time together on the weekends.

"I know it's hard, but I want you both to do something for me. I want you to do the very best you can at school and trust me to take care of things and know that I will do the right thing for all of us. Can you please do that for me? Do we have a deal?"

"We have a deal," they both agreed.

I looked at David. I put my hand on his shoulder. "David, that means no worrying, okay, Son?"

"Okay, Dad, I will try."

I told them we would go camping that weekend. I knew it would help to have something fun planned to look forward to.

I took them home and hugged them extra tight and extra long that night. I stayed with them until they fell asleep. Then I went into the bedroom to pack some clothes. Nikki sat on the bed. Neither of us spoke.

Rick and Linda were already in bed when I got to their house. There was a note for me on the door. It said, 'The door is open and the guest room is all yours. Make yourself at home and you are welcome here for as long as you want to stay.'

They were good friends.

A Long Distance Connection

"Hi Dad, what's going on? What has you so upset today?" David stared at his dad's face. Was there an expression on his face? Maybe a grimace? "Are you in any pain?" Chris was right. It was subtle, but something was definitely different.

David sat down by the bed and took his dad's hand and wrapped it around his. "I miss you, Dad. I'll try to fill you in on what all has been going on.

"Allison has grown since you last saw her. You are right…they grow up so fast. She misses her Pap, you know. I can't wait for you to see her again. I told her I was coming to see you and she sends a big hug and lots of kisses.

"We got all the money sent in for Charlie's basketball camps this summer. The coaches are planning to keep him busy, it seems." He wouldn't mention that Charlie was refusing to go anywhere for the summer. David knew that would upset his Dad, but he also couldn't blame Charlie because he felt the exact same way. No way was he going anywhere and leaving his father.

He thought about the conversation he and Chris had earlier. He was not only thankful for the good years with his mom, he was also thankful that his parents had finally been able to enjoy some good years together, too.

He thought about how hard it would be for his dad to wake up and find out that his wife of thirty-one years was gone. He knew it would be important to him to know they had done everything exactly as she had wanted.

"We had a memorial service for Mom. It was nice, Dad. You would have been pleased. We carried out all her final wishes. Rick remembered the papers that were in your safe at work. It helped a lot that you and Mom took care of everything ahead of time."

David thought about the safe and all the papers he had come across that day.

"Dad, there was an old letter in the safe written to you from Grandfather Hughes. I would like to read it one day if you don't mind."

He then thought about the envelope with the South Carolina address and the picture of the mystery woman inside.

"Oh yea, Dad, there was an envelope in there with an address from South Carolina on the front. There was a picture inside of an attractive girl probably in her mid to late twenties. She had beautiful green eyes. I have been wondering about her. The name on the back of the picture was Brooke."

David felt his father's hand slowly tighten around his. He looked down in disbelief.

"Dad?"

He wondered if he should call for the nurses. His dad's hand had now gone limp around his. He knew they would tell him it was nothing more than a tightening of the muscles in his hand. But David was convinced that it was something more.

He lay his head down on the bed, his hand still inside his dad's hand, and he wept. He was exhausted. He fell asleep.

"How was the camping trip?" Rick asked.

"It was fun. It seemed to do us all some good."

The boys and I had spent the whole weekend together on a camping trip and I had taken them home late the day before. It was Monday morning and I had gone back over to the house to pick them up and take them to school.

"Rick, I am going to start looking for a place today."

"John, you know you can stay at the house. You aren't even there except to sleep. Besides, it will be expensive keeping up two places."

"Thanks, Rick, but I really do need to find my own place."

Rick knew that John was a proud man, and yes, a stubborn man, and he knew it would do no good to argue with him about it. Once he had his mind made up, there was no changing it.

"Wait a minute...why don't you stay here?"

"Huh? Stay here?"

"Yea, Dad used to sleep here in the early years when he was putting in so many long hours. We already have a kitchen and bathroom, and Dad used to have a bed in the empty storage area in the back. He slept here those nights he worked late and was too tired to make the long drive home."

"That would be perfect, Rick. I can get a bed and a television and I will have everything I need. Are you sure you won't mind me staying here at the office?"

"Why would I mind? Linda and I even have a bed in storage that you can use."

That afternoon, Rick and I went to get the bed and brought it back to the office and set it up in the empty storage room. We then went and bought a television and radio and a night table and chair. We got some supplies for the kitchen and bathroom.

"There, just like home," I said as I put the rug down we had picked out for the room. "I will be just fine here. And the price is right. Thanks, Rick, this was a great idea."

I went over to get the boys and take them out to eat. I told them about the room Rick and I had fixed at the office. They wanted to see it, so we drove over and sat and watched some television before I took them home.

"Can we bring our sleeping bags over and camp out with you here sometime, Dad?" Chris wanted to know.

"Absolutely, Son. We will do that real soon."

I couldn't sleep. The bed was comfortable, but I couldn't get everything off my mind. I tossed and turned and finally got out of bed and sat in the chair. I turned on the television. I flipped channels and couldn't find anything I wanted to watch.

I went to my desk and turned my computer on. I thought about the website that Rick had shown me the week before.

"Come look at this, John," he had said. "They have these chat rooms that you can go into and you are connected to people from all over the world. It's amazing."

He showed me how you could choose a topic that was of interest to you. I found the site and followed the instructions for setting up a screen name. There was a list of subjects being discussed in each room. I decided to go into a chat room where they were talking about music.

Rick was right...it was amazing. There were fifty or so people in that one room sharing ideas and expressing their opinions on the latest music and artists. Each person had a screen name, and it was fascinating just sitting there and reading the names that everyone had come up with.

There was a box on the side of the screen showing who was coming into the room and who was leaving. There was continuous typing. Some had a lot to say and others sat quietly and observed as I did.

I was getting sleepy and just about to leave the room when another box came up at the top of my computer screen. The box was labeled private message. Someone had typed the word 'Hi'.

I was amused that someone had sent me a personal message. I responded by typing the word 'Hi' back to the person who had sent it to me.

'A/S/L' appeared on the screen. I didn't know what that meant, so I typed in a big question mark.

There was a response. 'I'll go first. I am asking your age, your sex, and your location. I see you are new at this. I am 28/female/from South Carolina.'

"Oh, these computer chatters have a language all their own," I thought. I was fascinated. "This new computer generation has a whole new means of communication."

'Oh, I see. I am 33/male/from Montana. And yes, I am new at this.'

'Are you married?' she typed.

'Yes.'

'Well, this is a first. An honest man. Most of the guys on here don't admit to being married.'

I read her words. I typed back to her... 'Well, I might as well be honest. I am very much married. There's not much getting around that.'

'You said you are new at this. I am curious as to why you came into this chat room tonight.'

'I have moved away from home for awhile. I guess maybe out of boredom and also a little out of curiosity.'

'And what do you think about your first chat room?'

'I think I like.'

'I like your sense of humor. It is refreshing to talk to someone like you.'

I found myself curious about this 28 year old female from South Carolina. I wanted to know more about her. I wasn't too sure of chat room etiquette, but I figured if she could ask my marital status, that it would be okay for me to do the same.

'Are you married?'

'No.'

'Have a boyfriend?'

'Yes, he is serving in the army. He's overseas right now. Do you have any children?'

'Yes, I have two boys. What about you?'

'Yes, I have one son. By the way, my name is Brooke.'

I wondered if the boyfriend overseas was the father of her son. I wondered a lot of things about this stranger from South Carolina two thousand miles away. I wondered what her life was like there.

'You said you have moved away from home. I hope you don't mind me asking...I was wondering why.'

'No, that's fine. You can ask me anything you like. I am separated right now. Long story.'

'Well, I hope I get to hear it sometime. Oh my goodness, it's late. I have to get up early in the morning. I have to say goodnight. I hope we can chat again sometime.'

'I would like that,' I typed to her. 'Goodnight, Brooke.'

'Goodnight...I don't know your name.'

'My name is John.'

'Goodnight, John.'

I turned off the computer and sat and stared at the blank screen. I didn't know why I had gone into that chat room. It was not something I would normally do. And with all the different rooms available, and the hundreds of people coming and going into each one, I didn't know why I had somehow connected to that one particular person in South Carolina.

I had long ago stopped believing in chance. I had learned that everything that happens seems to happen for a reason. I have thought back to that first meeting with Brooke many times. *Was it fate? Was it destiny? Was it a meeting of two lonely souls who at that very moment in time very much needed each other?* I didn't know the answer. I also couldn't have known that night that after the unlikely meeting of this Montana boy and that South Carolina girl, my life would never again be the same.

I leaned back in my chair and realized how relaxed I felt. It had been a long time since I'd been able to get my problems off my mind. Yes, I hoped our paths would cross again real soon.

Getting to Know You

I picked the boys up from school the next afternoon and took them home. Nikki had left a note saying she was at her mom's. I told the boys to get started on their homework.

I went into the bedroom and packed some more of my clothes and took them to the car. The house was clean. Mimi was not getting around as good as she used to, and she had hired someone to help clean her house. She had mentioned to Nikki earlier that she would bring her over one day to give our place a good, thorough cleaning. I figured she must have done just that.

I wondered if Mimi and the 'Colonel' had been told that I wasn't living at home. I hadn't spoken to Nikki since the morning of the coffee incident.

I played a video game with David and helped Chris get his homework finished and then took them to a junior high basketball game. They wanted to eat hotdogs and nachos at the game for their dinner. "Okay," I told them, "but tomorrow night we are going to have some vegetables."

Chris laughed. "Dad, didn't you know a kid my age can live off of junk?"

"That may be," I answered him. "But just in case, we are going to get some fruits and vegetables down you, too."

I was keeping a close eye on both Chris and David. They seemed to be adjusting well to our new living arrangement. I was trying to

147

keep our schedules and our time together as close to how it had always been as possible. Except for sleeping under different roofs, things had not changed very much for us.

They hadn't mentioned their mom's and my situation since that first day I told them I was leaving, and I was glad. I needed some time. It had only been a week. I didn't want to rush things. I didn't want to make such an important, life-changing decision that affected all of us until I was absolutely sure what was best.

Nikki was home when we pulled up after the game. I walked the boys to the door and saw her standing in the kitchen. I said goodnight and hugged them and left.

I got back to the office a little after nine. I immediately turned on the computer and went into the same music chat room I had been in the night before. I recognized some of the same screen names, and there were some new ones, too. I looked for Brooke. She wasn't there.

I waited around about fifteen minutes. *This is crazy, John. What are the chances that you will run into that same girl in here again? Besides, even if you do, she will more than likely want to meet and talk to someone new.*

I was about to leave the room when I saw her screen name appear. Brooke had entered the room. I smiled when I saw her name.

This time, I am the one who sent the private message. 'Hi.'

'Well, hi yourself,' she typed back to me. 'I am surprised to see you back here again tonight.'

I wondered if I should dare tell her she was the reason I had come back tonight. *Why not?* 'I was hoping I might run into you again.'

'You know, I was hoping that same thing,' she typed.

She continued. 'So, John, how was your day?'

I looked at the screen. Six simple words. This sweet girl from South Carolina who didn't know me from Adam was asking me how my day was. How easy that would have been for Nikki to do. But she never asked. She never asked because she didn't care. Somehow, I got the feeling that Brooke really did care about my day.

'I actually had a good day, Brooke. Thanks for asking. And how was your day?'

She told me that her day had been trying, but rewarding. I wondered what that meant.

'Let's talk,' I typed.

'What about?' she asked.

'About you. I want to know about Brooke.'

'And just what do you want to know about me?'

'I want to know everything about you that you are willing to share with me.'

'Okay. You are a brave soul...here goes...'

I smiled and leaned back in my chair as she started typing and telling me about her life.

'You already know that I am 28 years old and I live in SC. I have lived here for my entire life. I am a first grade school teacher...'

That explains her day being trying, but rewarding. The girl has the patience of Job if she spends her days in a classroom full of first graders.

'I am a single mom. I have a little boy who is three years old named Ben. He is the love of my life, and he keeps me on my toes.'

'Yes, they can sure be a handful at that age. I was wondering...' I stopped typing.

'Wondering what?' she asked.

'Nothing...it's none of my business.'

'John, I really enjoy chatting with you. What do you think about us establishing a rule right here and now that we can talk about anything we want to talk about and we can ask about anything we want to ask about. If the other person doesn't want to talk about a certain subject or answer a certain question, then he or she can just say so.'

'I like that rule, Brooke. Okay, I was wondering about Ben's father.'

'I thought you might be,' she typed. 'And I don't mind talking to you about that a bit. I fell for the wrong guy my senior year of college. I really did think he was the one, but boy, was I wrong! I got pregnant and he took off. He has not been in my life or the life of his son at all since then.'

I sat there and thought about my boys. I couldn't believe a man could turn his back on a woman having his child. I especially couldn't believe he could turn his back on his own son. 'I am sorry.'

'It's okay...really,' she told me. 'We are better off without him. And I am very lucky. My mama lives close and she is a big help. I don't know what I would do without her. She keeps Ben during the day while I am at school.'

I was glad to know she had some help. 'And your dad?'

'He's been dead since I was a little girl. I don't remember him.'

They say that everyone has a story, and I found myself interested in each and every word as Brooke shared hers with me.

'Now tell me about the 'military' man.'

'Military man, huh. John, you make me smile. His name is Gregory. I met him about a year ago. He was stationed at a nearby military base and someone set us up on a blind date. We started going together soon after that. He was deployed to overseas duty about three months ago.'

'Tell me about him.' I was curious to know what kind of man had caught Brooke's eye.

'Well, let's see…Gregory is a good man. He's been in the army for his entire adult life. He is thirty-five years old. He has never been married and doesn't have any children, but he is great with Ben. And that means a lot to me. And he is also very good to me.'

She continued, 'And now you are wondering what a school teacher with a three year old son and a boyfriend is doing talking to strange men on the computer.'

I laughed out loud. 'Well, no, I haven't wondered that. But now that you mention it, what IS a school teacher with a three year old son and a boyfriend doing talking to strange men on the computer?' I imagined Brooke sitting in her house in SC laughing, too.

'Like you said last night, I'm probably a little bored and a little curious. I try to have Ben in bed by eight-thirty each night, and I guess I get a little lonely at times. It's nice to meet people. And it is especially nice to meet someone who is as easy to talk to as you.'

I thought about Brooke's situation…she was still so young and had the responsibility of raising a three year old boy alone. And now with her boyfriend stationed overseas, I was sure that she did get quite lonely.

'Brooke, you seem to be such a sweet person. It is especially nice to meet you, too. I have to tell you something…'

'I'm listening,' she said.

'I couldn't sleep last night. That's why I got up and turned the computer on. After we talked and said goodnight, I was relaxed for the first time in a long time, and I was able to lie down afterwards and get a good night's sleep. I really enjoy talking to you.'

'I'm glad, John. Gregory gave me his computer before he left, and I've been coming into chat rooms for a couple of months now, but I haven't really met anyone who I cared to talk to for very long until last night.'

'Okay, turnabout is fair play. It's your turn.'

'My turn?'

'Yes, I want to know all about John.'

'Okay…ready or not, here goes,' I typed. 'I grew up near Chicago, but I have been living in Montana since the eleventh grade.'

'Why did you move?' she asked.

'My parents died and I came here to live with my aunt and uncle.'

'Oh John, I am so sorry.'

I suspected Brooke was wondering about the circumstances of their deaths, but she didn't ask and I figured that was better left to discuss another day.

'Anyway, I started going with this girl in school and she got pregnant our senior year. We got married and my first boy, David, was born. Then four years later, my second son, Chris, was born. They are growing up so fast. David is fifteen now and Chris is eleven. I have two fine boys.'

'Spoken like a proud father,' she said.

'Brooke, I have been blessed with two of the finest sons any man could have. Yes, I am so proud.

'I am in the real estate business. Nikki…that's my wife…and I have been having some problems for a long time now, and believe it or not, I am actually living at the office. I am sitting at my desk typing to you from my work computer.

'I have stayed in a bad marriage all these years because of the boys. But they are getting older now, and I realize we are not doing them any favors by staying together in an unhappy situation.'

'Do you get to see them much?' she wanted to know.

'Oh yea, I go over every morning to take them to school and I pick them up every afternoon. We went camping this past weekend.'

'John, you are a great dad.'

'I sure try to be.' I looked at my watch. 'Well, I have kept you up past your bedtime again. It's almost eleven.'

'Did you forget about the time zones? I am on the east coast. It's two hours later here. It's almost one o'clock in the morning here.'

'Oh man, Brooke, I am so sorry. I wasn't even thinking about that. You will be dragging in the morning.'

'It's alright...I will be fine. I enjoyed talking to you again. I know it's late, but I still wish we didn't have to say goodnight.'

I knew exactly what she meant. I didn't want to say goodnight, either. But we did, and this time I felt confident that we would be talking again real soon. I was again relaxed and again able to get a good night's sleep.

For the next couple of weeks, we were on the computer together every chance we got. I found myself thinking about her more and more. I looked forward to being with her and always hated when it was time to say goodnight.

The more I knew about Brooke, the more I wanted to know. I didn't mind all the typing, but it was slow and frustrating trying to get everything said we wanted to say in the short amount of time we had. I began to wonder how she would feel about giving me her phone number. It would be so much easier to talk on the telephone. Besides, I wanted to hear her voice.

Call Me

I made the decision going back to the office that next night that I would ask Brooke if I could call her. She was already online waiting for me when I went into our chat room.

'Well, there you are,' she typed. 'I have missed you.'

She always made me smile. 'I have missed you, too.'

'So, tell me about your day.'

I told her all about my day. I then told her I had a question for her.

'Shoot,' she said.

'Well, I will ask, and the worst that can happen is you can say no, right?'

'Right. You now have me curious, John. So ask away.'

I explained to Brooke that I didn't mind the typing, but that we always had so much we wanted to talk about and so little time. I then told her I had been wondering if it would be okay if I called her sometime.

'That's a great idea, John, but not an original one. I have been thinking the exact same thing. Besides, I would love to hear your voice.'

I was smiling again. 'And why didn't you mention it?' I asked.

'A long distance phone call costs money, Silly. I wasn't going to ask you to spend your hard-earned money to call me.'

That was just like Brooke to be considerate of someone else. 'You let me worry about that. I would love to call you sometime.'

Her phone number appeared on the screen. I asked her when it would be a good time to call.

'How about now?' she asked.

'Is Ben asleep? I don't want to disturb him.'

'Yes, but he is a sound sleeper. I have the ringer turned down low and it won't disturb him at all.'

'Okay, I am about to call.'

'John, I am a little nervous.'

'Me, too. But excited. I can't believe I am about to hear your voice for the very first time.'

I picked up the phone and dialed Brooke's number. My hands were shaking. She picked up on the second ring.

"Hello," she said.

"Hello to you, too," I answered.

"John, it is so good to finally hear your voice."

"Oh my gosh…" I couldn't believe what I was hearing. "Brooke… your voice…"

"Okay Mister, are you going to make fun of the way I talk now? I am from South Carolina, remember? We do speak like this down here, you know."

I began to laugh as Brooke defended her Southern accent. "No, Angel, you don't understand. My mom was from Georgia, and even though she moved to Illinois, she never lost her Southern accent. You sound like her, Brooke. You say my name like she said it. You sound familiar to me. I love your voice."

Brooke was laughing now, too. Her laugh was warm and contagious and made me feel good inside. "Oh John, I am glad. And I love your voice, too. It's just as I had imagined it to be."

"This is much better," I said. "I like to be able to talk to you and not have all that typing to do."

"Yes, it is. But I don't want you to have an expensive phone bill."

"Don't you worry about that, Brooke. Just talk to me."

And talk is what we did. We spent three or more hours each night on the phone. We talked about anything and everything. No subject was off limits. I was surprised at how much we thought alike and how much we had in common.

She wanted to know everything there was to know about my childhood and my years growing up in Chicago. She wanted to know all about my mom and my dad. She listened carefully to every little detail and asked questions if she felt I had left anything out.

"Oh John, your dad sounds like the best dad ever. And your mom sounds like a wonderful mother and quite a fascinating lady. No wonder you turned out to be such a nice man. You were raised right. I know you miss them."

"I do miss them a lot. I am constantly reminded of them and the things they taught me growing up."

It felt good to talk about those years to someone who really wanted to hear about them. Brooke asked about everything going on in my life. She wanted to hear about the little things such as what I had for breakfast and if I'd had a good night's sleep. And she wanted to know about the big things…my hopes and my dreams and all those things that were important to me.

I asked about her childhood. I told her I was sorry she had lost her dad so young and had to grow up without him.

"I had a good childhood, John," she said. "Even without my daddy, my mama made sure I didn't miss out on anything."

Brooke told me all about her childhood and her years growing up in South Carolina. She told me that she and her mom had always been very close. "I don't know what I would do without her," she said. "She always sticks by me through thick and thin."

"I would love to meet your mom someday, Brooke. She has to be a fine lady to have raised such a special girl."

"What a sweet thing to say," she said. "John, I feel so close to you tonight."

"I feel close to you tonight, too, Brooke." The truth was that I didn't know anyone like her existed in the world, and I was developing some very strong feelings for her.

Brooke loved hearing stories about the 'Colonel'.

"I thought people like that could only be seen in the movies," she would say.

When I told her the 'Colonel' used to let Nikki go to a dress shop and buy any outfit she pleased, Brooke would listen in disbelief. "That man ruined her, John."

"Tell me about it," I said. "Nikki has no concept of the value of a dollar. It has been a constant struggle keeping her on a budget. I finally had to put her on an allowance."

"You put her on an allowance?" Brooke asked in amazement. "You actually gave a grown woman an allowance?"

"I had to. If I hadn't, she would have put us in the poor house. But to tell you the truth, it did very little good. She still slipped around and bought things and tried to hide them from me."

Brooke sat in silence for a few moments. She had been raising a son alone on a teacher's salary and had learned how to stretch a dollar and get by on very little. She and Ben didn't have a lot of extras, but they had everything they needed, and she seemed content with that.

"You don't have a wife," she finally said. "You have an extra child to raise."

There was more truth to her statement than she even knew. I then told her about the morning I had found the clothes in the sack in the closet and asked her to take them back; about Nikki throwing a hot cup of coffee on me and telling me she hated me in front of the boys. "That was the day I finally left."

"What are you going to do, John? Are you going to go back to her?"

I thought about her questions. I hadn't known the answers to those questions until now. "No, I'm not going back. It's over between Nikki and me."

I felt a great sense of relief. I had known all along that things weren't going to get any better. To go back into that same situation wouldn't be fair to any of us. It was time to admit our marriage was over and to move on.

I was driving back to the office. It was a beautiful, clear night in Montana. The moon was full. I called Brooke when I walked inside. "Are the skies clear in South Carolina tonight?" I asked.

"Yes, they are," she said as she looked out the window.

"Do you see that full moon tonight, Brooke?"

156

"Yes, I see it. It's beautiful."

I told Brooke what my mom used to say when the moon was full. "Look at that, John. Look close. Can you see that big ole moon smiling down at you?"

"Yes, Mom, I can see it," I would tell her looking up into the sky.

Then she would say... "I see the moon and the moon sees me. God bless the moon and God bless John and me."

Brooke loved that she could look at the same moon in South Carolina that I was looking at in Montana. She said it somehow made the miles between us seem not so far and that it made her feel closer to me.

"I don't even know what you look like, Brooke, and I don't even care. You are the most beautiful, special person I have ever known. The more I get to know you, the more I like and respect you."

"Would you like to see a picture of me, John?"

"Oh yes, I would very much like to see a picture of you."

Brooke told me to go to my email account and she would send one. "The one I'm sending was just taken a couple of weeks ago when we had Mama's birthday party."

I sat and anxiously waited for the email to come in with the picture of Brooke. When it finally came, I opened it up and looked at the attached photo. I sat and stared at the picture on my screen.

"Oh man, Brooke, you are so very beautiful."

"So, you aren't disappointed?" she asked.

"Angel, there's no way I would have been disappointed. I fell in love with you a long time ago. And the fact that you are just as beautiful on the outside as you are on the inside is just icing on the cake."

"John, that is so sweet."

I kept staring at the picture. She had long, thick brown hair and the most gorgeous green eyes I had ever seen. She had a smile that made my heart melt. She looked to be of medium height and had a very nice build.

"Brooke...I hope you don't mind me saying this..."

"Uh oh, come on, tell me..."

"Girl, you are some kind of hot!"

I could hear her laughing. "No, I don't mind you saying that at all. So, you like?"

"Yes, I very much like. Brooke, I am so very attracted to you, Angel."

"I am glad," she replied. "But not fair...I don't know what you look like."

"I will get you a picture, I promise."

We talked awhile about our favorite subject...our boys. I kept staring at the picture.

I suddenly remembered the website that had the listings of the real estate firms in our area. Rick and I had paid to advertise on it and had sent in our pictures for our ad. I told Brooke the name of the website so she could go there to see my picture.

I now knew how she felt when she was waiting for me to see her picture. I was nervous and hoping that she wouldn't be too disappointed. "Are you there yet?" I asked.

"Not yet." She laughed. "But almost. I can't wait to see it."

I continued to sit there and wait.

"Okay, I found it."

She wasn't saying anything. "What are you doing?" I finally asked.

"I am sitting here looking at the most handsome man I ever did see. John David Hughes, Jr., huh? I like the name. And I also like the man. You've been holding out on me, you know. You didn't tell me you were this good looking."

I suspected Brooke was exaggerating more than just a bit, but I still sat there with a big smile on my face. "Are you serious or are you messing with me?" I finally asked.

"John, what I love most about our relationship is that we are always so honest with each other. And I can honestly tell you that I am so very attracted to you, too. And I wish there weren't so many miles between us."

I knew exactly what Brooke was saying. I wanted to be with her. I hadn't realized until I got to know her how many walls I had built around my feelings and emotions over the years to protect myself from getting hurt. And slowly, but surely, Brooke had started to tear down those walls, one by one. She understood me and accepted me just as I was. I felt safe with her and I began to trust her with my heart. I could sense she felt the same way.

"Well, it's late and I know you need to get to bed," I told her. "As always, I hate to say goodnight."

"John?"

"Yes?"

"John, you said something earlier…you said you loved me."

"I did?"

"Yes, you said you fell in love with me a long time ago."

I hadn't even realized that I had said the words. But since she liked the honesty, I was sure going to be honest now. "Brooke, I feel like I've known you my entire life. And sitting here right now talking to you, I can't even remember a time when I didn't love you. Loving you seems as natural to me as breathing. But I'm not a free man and I shouldn't have said that to you. I'm so sorry if I offended you."

Brooke told me that I had caught her off guard a bit, but that she never wanted me to apologize again for my feelings. She said she was always interested in knowing how I felt, and especially how I felt about her. "And besides," she said, "you aren't in this boat alone, you know. I have fallen fast and hard, too. Yes, I have lost my mind. I am in love with a man who I have never even met."

We both laughed and said goodnight. My last thought before I drifted off to sleep was of Brooke. *Yes, we really do need to do something about these miles between us.*

Wonderful Tonight

"Good morning, Rick."

"Good morning, John. Man, someone has been in a great mood lately. What's going on with you?"

I had wanted to tell Rick about Brooke, and this seemed to be the perfect time. "I've met someone, Rick."

Rick smiled. "You know, I suspected as much. But I couldn't figure out when you would have had time to be seeing someone."

"Well, I haven't actually met her."

Rick had a puzzled look on his face.

I tried to explain. "I couldn't sleep the first night I slept here at the office, and I went into that chat room you showed me on the computer. I met this girl named Brooke from South Carolina and we chatted for a couple of weeks on the computer, then I called her, then we traded pictures, and Rick, she is the most awesome girl I have ever known."

"Slow down, Buddy," he said with a hint of concern on his face. "So, this is a long distance relationship?"

I went to my computer and pulled up Brooke's picture. "This is Brooke."

"Wow, nice!" he said.

"Yes and we talk every night after I get back here from spending time with the boys. By the way, Rick, we will be getting a rather large phone bill this next time. Don't worry, because most of it will be my personal calls to Brooke, and I will reimburse the company for them."

Rick laughed. "I'm not worried about a big phone bill, John. I am just trying to make sense out of what you are telling me. I haven't seen you this excited in a long time."

I knew it had to be hard for Rick to understand what I was saying. "Rick, I know it hasn't been that long, but I am in love with Brooke. We have spent more time talking and probably know more about each other than most couples who have dated for a year or more. And I can't wait for you to meet her."

Rick looked at me. "Don't you want to meet her first?"

"You know what I mean," I said grinning. "And yes, I intend to do just that. Do you remember that brochure we got awhile back on that realtor's convention in Southern California?"

"Yes, I remember," he said.

"Well, I was thinking that maybe I should see if Brooke will agree to meet me there."

We had covered all the big subjects…politics, religion, world events. But there was one subject that we had never talked about and I wondered when it would come up. I decided that when it did, I would make sure it was Brooke who brought it up.

"What do you want to talk about, Brooke," I asked her. "What's in that pretty head of yours tonight?"

"I was curious about something," she said. "I want you to tell me about the first time you were intimate with someone."

I laughed. "I knew the subject would eventually come up, but I wasn't expecting it tonight."

She was surprised to know that I had never been with anyone but Nikki. She said she couldn't believe there was a man living in this world who had reached his thirties and who had only been with one woman.

"Well, it's true," I assured her. "I've only been with one woman my whole life, and that's Nikki."

"Okay, so tell me about your sex life with Nikki."

"What sex life?" I asked. "Nikki was never interested in being with me. Sex eventually became just another of her weapons of manipulation. She used it when she wanted something. The last time we were intimate was just a few weeks before I left home, and before that it had been longer than I can even remember."

I thought back to that night. "Yes, it was only because there was something that Nikki wanted. I don't know what that was, but I do know that it had nothing to do with wanting to be with her husband or wanting to satisfy my needs."

"You know, John, that may be more common in marriages than you think."

"You may be right," I said. "Now it's your turn."

Brooke told me that most of her friends had been sexually active in high school. "But my mama drilled in me from the time I was very young that there was to be no sex until marriage. And I fully intended to be a virgin when I married. Then I fell in love (or at least thought I did) with a guy at college. I wasn't planning on having sex, so I wasn't prepared, and when it happened, I got pregnant immediately."

Brooke paused. "Now that I look back, I realize that our whole relationship was nothing but a disaster from the start, but I didn't see that until it was too late. But you know, John, when I look at Ben, I don't have any regrets. I can't. I am too thankful to have him."

It didn't surprise me to hear my own words coming out of her mouth.

She began to talk about Gregory. I had tried to put this Gregory guy out of my mind as much as possible, but I had to face the fact that he was a reality in Brooke's life.

She said she had dated him for over six months before she ever slept with him. "This time you had better believe that I was both prepared and protected. So, I've been with two guys."

I had never had a jealous thought in my life, but I found myself getting jealous at the thought of Brooke with another man. I wondered how often she heard from Gregory and what her feelings were for him now that we had met and had gotten so close. I didn't ask. I didn't know if that was because I didn't feel it was right to ask, or if it was because I didn't really want to know.

"I want to know more about you," she said. "Tell me something else you enjoy that we haven't talked about yet. I know you love music and I know you love a nice, long drive with no particular destination... tell me something else, John."

I thought about her question for a moment. "Something else I enjoy...let's see...well, one of the more simple things I enjoy in life is a beautiful sunset." I told her how my dad had taught me to appreciate a sunset. "He said that whenever he saw a sunset, he would stop and take a deep breath and relax...that it always made him feel at peace... that no matter what was going on in his life, it reminded him that God was in control and that everything was going to be alright."

I told Brooke that he had passed that appreciation to me and I had tried to pass it on to my boys.

There was a pause on the other end of the line and then a deep sigh. "John, do you have any idea how much I would love to experience a sunset with you?"

I thought about what she said. The most peaceful image came to my mind...Brooke by my side...my arms around her...the smell of her hair...her beautiful eyes looking into mine, then at the sunset.

"Meet me in California, Brooke."

"Do what?" she laughed.

"There is a realtor's convention in Southern California. Meet me there."

She wanted to know all about it. I told her that it was at the end of the month.

"I will send you an airline ticket and I will be at the Los Angeles airport waiting on you when you arrive. We can rent a car and drive down the coastline to where the convention is in Newport Beach. You would be flying out on Friday and returning home on Sunday, so you wouldn't miss but one day of school. Could your mom keep Ben? Could it work, Brooke? Will you meet me in California?"

"It sounds wonderful, John. Will you let me think about it and see if it can be arranged?"

"Sure, take all the time you need. Just say the word and I will get the tickets purchased."

"I have never flown," she said.

"Never?" I asked.

"No, never."

"Are you afraid to fly?"

"Not at all. And knowing you will be at the other end of the flight makes it sound like the most exciting trip I could ever take."

Brooke had me smiling again. "Think about it, Brooke. Think about sitting out on the California coast as the sun sets over the Pacific Ocean."

"Get those tickets, John. I will make it work."

It was morning. I had already taken the boys to school and had gotten back to the office. "I couldn't sleep last night, Rick. Brooke said she will meet me in California."

Rick poured himself a cup of coffee and sat down by my desk.

I kept talking, much faster than usual. "She's never flown before. It's a long flight. I have a plan."

Rick smiled. He had never seen his friend so excited about anything except the birth of his sons. "And just what is this plan of yours?" he asked.

"Well, I have checked all the flights. Brooke will have a short flight from South Carolina to the Atlanta airport. She thinks I will be waiting for her in Los Angeles. But I am going to fly to Atlanta the night before. And I am going to purchase two first class tickets side by side from Atlanta to Los Angeles. When she gets on her flight in Atlanta, I will be sitting there beside her. Can you imagine the surprise on her face?"

Rick had to admit that it was a clever plan. "Not only will you surprise her, it will give you more time with her and also keep her from having to make that long flight alone."

"Oh man, Rick, I can't wait."

That night Brooke gave me the official word that she could make the trip. "I will line up a sub for that Friday and my mom said she will keep Ben that weekend. I didn't really lie to her, John, but I certainly didn't tell her the whole truth. I told her I was meeting a good friend that weekend. I'm sure she assumed I meant a female friend, and I let her assume just that." She laughed nervously. "I sure wasn't prepared to tell her all the details of this trip. Are you as excited as I am?"

"I am so excited until I can't sleep," I told her. "Your airline ticket will be waiting for you at the gate when you arrive at the airport that Friday morning. You will be making one plane change in Atlanta, and then there will be a direct flight to Los Angeles."

"And you will really be waiting for me in Los Angeles, John? I will finally get to meet you?"

"You will finally get to meet me," I said. "Oh, and Brooke...don't you worry...I have booked us two hotel rooms. I know how 'proper' you Southern ladies are. I know you don't ever kiss on the first date."

She laughed and said, "You are so bad, John David Hughes. What am I going to do with you? And just for your information, I don't consider this our first date. This is more like the fiftieth date, I do believe."

"Do you know how much you make me smile?" I asked her. "And just for your information, I got adjoining rooms."

When Brooke and I talked that Wednesday night before our trip, I told her goodnight and that I was headed to the airport the following day and I would see her in Los Angeles when she landed on Friday. "Have a safe flight, Angel."

I flew to Atlanta on Thursday and stayed at a hotel near the airport. I was up bright and early on Friday morning getting ready for my trip to the airport and my very first meeting with Brooke.

I caught a taxi to the airport and got on the plane as soon as it was cleared for boarding. I sat down in my first class seat next to the window. I could feel my heart pounding in my chest as the passengers walked down the aisle to their seats.

I took the newspaper I had bought that morning and opened it and pretended to be reading it so my face would be covered. She finally sat down in the seat next to me.

It was all I could do not to say something to her right then and there, but I decided to have a little fun first. I moved my leg over until it touched hers. I felt her move her leg away immediately. I imagined how uncomfortable that had made her and I was trying not to laugh.

I then took my hand and placed it on her left leg right above her knee. She reached for my hand to move it away, and I grabbed her hand and held onto it.

"Sir, I don't appreciate..."

I couldn't hold back the laughter any longer. "You sure do smell good," I interrupted her as I slowly put the paper down. "Please continue...you don't appreciate..."

Brooke was about to get up. She sat back in her seat and slowly turned to face me. Her eyes met mine. "John? John, is it really you?"

"Yes, Brooke, it's really me." She was even more beautiful in person. She had high cheekbones and smooth skin. She smiled at me and it took my breath away. I was looking into the most gorgeous green eyes I had ever seen. They were the color of emeralds. I could feel my eyes light up as I looked at her.

Brooke sat back in her seat as she tried to get over the shock of seeing me there. "I don't know whether to hug you or kill you," she said. "I was about to ask the stewardess to move me to another seat. I was thinking that it was just my luck to have to take my first airplane ride sitting next to the world's biggest pervert."

We both laughed and I took Brooke into my arms and held her close to me. I couldn't get over how beautiful she was. She wore a simple black dress that fit her well and was slightly low in the front. Her body was firm and well proportioned.

I took her hands in mine. They were shaking. I didn't know if she was more nervous about our first meeting or about her first flight. I asked her.

"John, I wasn't expecting to see you until I arrived in Los Angeles. This is a lot to take in all at once. I am very nervous and also very excited right now. I can't believe I am sitting here with you next to me. I just need a little time to settle down."

I smiled at Brooke and kissed her on the cheek. I looked deep into her eyes and held her hands until they stopped shaking. "I love you, Angel," I told her. "You are so very beautiful."

"I love you, too, John," she said. She was smiling back at me.

I stood up to put my briefcase and the newspaper in the overhead baggage compartment. I looked down and smiled at her again as I stepped over her feet and into the aisle of the airplane.

Brooke watched closely as he moved past her and stretched his body upward to open the overhead compartment. She noticed that he was wearing jeans and a crisp, white Oxford cloth buttoned-down shirt. He was tall and muscular and she liked the way he looked in his jeans. His hair was dark and his eyes were brown and he was even more handsome in person than in the picture she had seen of him.

I sat back down in my seat and leaned over close to her. "Fiftieth date, huh? Isn't that what you said?"

"Yes, at least the fiftieth."

I leaned over and kissed Brooke. It was a long, slow kiss that I didn't want to end. Her kiss tasted sweet, as I knew it would. The 'fasten your seatbelt' sign came on and I held her hand as our plane took off into the air.

We were soon as relaxed and comfortable with each other as we had always been when talking on the computer and on the phone. We talked all the way to California and the flight seemed over in no time. I knew that the whole weekend would pass just that fast.

When we landed, we rented a car and drove down the California coastline to our hotel. We checked in and went to our rooms. I had reserved adjoining suites with balconies that overlooked the beach and the ocean.

The spacious rooms had terrazzo floors and there was an ornate king-sized bed, a lush leather sofa and chair, and a mahogany entertainment center in each one. There were beautiful scenic paintings of the ocean and the rocky hills and cliffs along the beach hanging on the walls.

"The rooms are beautiful," Brooke said.

"Yes, they are," I said as I checked out the room.

"What's the plan?"

"What would you like to do first?" I asked her.

Brooke walked to her bathroom and looked inside the door.

"Wow, come and look at this, John."

The huge, white marbled bathrooms had mirrored walls and a Jacuzzi.

"I think I would like to get showered and changed and go out for an early dinner and maybe a walk on the beach," she said.

"I like that plan."

I went into my bathroom and showered and put on some white boxers. I got my cd player out of my suitcase and put an Eric Clapton cd in. I took it into my room and set it on the nightstand by the bed. I went back into the bathroom to blow dry my hair.

As I walked out of the bathroom, 'Wonderful Tonight' began to play. The door between our rooms was standing open and Brooke was standing in the doorway in a white silk robe. She had showered and her long, brown hair was almost dry.

"I love that song," she said.

I went to her and put my arms around her. I took my hand and gently ran it through her soft, silky hair. I leaned over and whispered softly in her ear. "I love you, Sweetheart." Then I started singing ever so quietly with the cd...'Oh my darling, you look wonderful tonight.'

I pulled Brooke close to me and our bodies began to slowly move to the music playing. I began to softly kiss her neck and kissed my way slowly to her lips.

"I've never felt this way before, John." Her voice was soft.

Our bodies continued to move in rhythm to the music. The song was ending. "You do look so wonderful, Brooke." She smiled at me as another song began to play. I continued to hold her tight and marveled at how close I felt to her.

We walked to the balcony just as the sun was beginning to set over the Pacific Ocean. We stood there; my arms wrapped around her, and watched our first sunset together.

"Your dad was right," she said. "There is nothing more relaxing than a sunset."

We ordered room service that night and listened to music and lay in bed and talked. I propped my head up on my hand and carefully studied Brooke's face as she talked. I slowly traced the sensual curve of her lips with my finger. I leaned over and kissed her and we made love. We finally drifted off to sleep.

We dressed early the next morning and went for a walk on the beach. We stopped at a little coffee shop along the way and got a cup of coffee and some banana nut muffins.

We found a quiet spot and a couple of chairs and sat in the sand near the ocean. I held Brooke's hand as she looked out across the vast ocean.

"Tell me what you are thinking right now."

"I am thinking that I would love to feel just like I feel right this very moment for the rest of my life," she said.

"I know exactly what you mean. I love this, Brooke. I love being here with you. It all feels so right."

I leaned over and kissed her. "I love you so much."

"I love you, too, John."

"I will tell you something if you promise not to laugh. It's something that no one else knows." I winked at her.

"I promise not to laugh," she said leaning closer.

"There's something I think about a lot…something I would love to do. I guess you could call it a fantasy of mine. I would love to someday spend my entire summer in a little cottage by the sea…spend each morning just as we've spent this one…an early morning walk along the beach…a cup of coffee in the cool of the morning…my bare feet in the sand…the sounds of the waves as they crash against the shore…a warm sea breeze blowing the smell of the salty seawater ashore.

"I want to write a book, Brooke. They say that everyone has at least one good novel in them. I want to sit on the front porch of that cottage by the sea and write my story as I look out over the ocean. I know it sounds crazy, and I know it will never happen, but it's something I dream about."

"No, it doesn't sound crazy. It sounds wonderful, John. I hope you can do that someday. Can I come?"

I laughed. "Sure, you can come. I like the sound of that. And don't forget about those sunsets at the end of each day."

"Ah, those sunsets," she said.

Tears streamed down both our faces as we held each other and kissed goodbye. It was time for Brooke to board her plane back to Atlanta. It had been a perfect weekend, but had gone by way too fast.

We had gone shopping the day before. While she was looking inside an antique shop, I had gone to a nearby jewelry store and found a beautiful gold angel necklace. I had it engraved and gift-wrapped.

We had a seafood dinner at a restaurant on the bay. We listened to live music and danced and talked about all the good times we would have together in the future.

I handed Brooke her present. She opened it and read the engraving on the angel. 'To Brooke, my angel…Always and Forever, John.' She cried as I put the gold angel around her neck.

"Just right," I said as I fastened the chain. "See how it falls next to your heart? You are my angel, Brooke, and I want this necklace to always remind you of how much I love you and that no matter where I am, my heart will always belong to you."

"How in the world am I going to get on that plane and go home without you tomorrow?" I asked her as we lay in each other's arms that night.

I watched as her plane took off and disappeared into the eastern sky. I walked to my gate and waited until time to board my plane back to Montana.

I didn't know I could feel this much love for anyone other than my kids. But I am totally and completely in love with Brooke, and I know without a doubt that I want to spend the rest of my life with her.

But John, even though your heart is with Brooke, you are not a free man. You know what you have to do. When you get home, you have to talk to Nikki. You have to tell her that it's time to get a divorce and move on with our lives.

She will be relieved to finally put an end to an unhappy marriage. She is still young and beautiful and she will meet someone who can make her happy. I want that for her.

I want the boys to live with me, and I know that's what they will want, too. Once they get to know Brooke, they will love her as much as I do.

Nikki won't have to worry about them and she can live her life as she's always wanted to live it. She will be free of the responsibilities that come with having a family.

I will assure Nikki that I will be more than fair in our divorce settlement. It's the right thing to do. It's the best thing for all of us.

My plane took off for Montana. I thought about Brooke. My heart welled with emotion.

I met her, Mom. I finally met the one who makes my eyes light up every time I look at her.

I leaned back in my seat.

Yes, it's time. I will talk to Nikki when I get home.

Awakenings

David awoke. He lifted his head off the bed. His neck was sore. He looked at his watch. He had been asleep for over an hour. The sheets were damp from his tears.

He thought about what had happened earlier. Had he overreacted? Maybe that was what the doctors had meant when they warned them of false hope.

He got up and stretched. He walked around the room and then back to the bed. He looked closely at his dad's face. He looked peaceful...as if he was having a restful sleep.

He again thought about his dad grasping his hand. He had been telling him about Allison and about Mom's memorial service...then about the safe...and then the letter...and then the picture. He remembered the last words he had spoken.

He leaned over and placed his cheek on his dad's cheek.

"Dad, who is Brooke?"

David stood up straight. He looked at his dad in amazement. "Dad? Dad, can you hear me? Oh God...please..."

He ran to the other side of the bed and pushed the call button. He ran over to his travel bag and fumbled around in it until he found his cell phone, never taking his eyes off his father.

He dialed Chris's number. His brother answered.

"Chris, get Charlie and come to the hospital. It's Dad…Chris, his eyes are open."

"Well, don't you look like the cat that swallowed the canary? How was the convention?"

"I can assure you I wasn't studying any convention."

Rick laughed. "How was your weekend, John?"

"It was a perfect weekend. The only complaint I have is that it had to end. Brooke is amazing, Rick."

I told Rick all about the trip and about the prank I had pulled on the plane. "She said it was just her luck to be on her very first plane ride sitting by the world's biggest pervert." I couldn't think about it without laughing.

Rick was laughing so hard until he was holding his side. "Did you really do that to the poor girl, John?"

"Yes, I did, and she was a great sport about the whole thing. I tell you, Man, I can't stand being away from her. I have made the decision that I am going to ask Nikki for a divorce. Why keep putting off the inevitable?"

"When are you going to do it?"

"I was thinking about that. Uncle Sid has talked about taking the boys fishing. I thought maybe we could arrange that this weekend. That will give Nikki and me some time alone to talk."

I went over to the house that next Saturday morning to get the boys up and ready for their fishing trip. I fixed breakfast and Uncle Sid pulled up while we were eating.

"Come in and have some breakfast," I told him.

"Thanks, but I have already had breakfast," he said. "Are you boys about ready?"

David and Chris got up and picked up their bags. I walked with them to the truck. "You boys have fun and mind Uncle Sid. And don't catch all of them."

Uncle Sid laughed. "We'll try to leave a few in the lake."

"I wish you were going with us, Dad," Chris said.

"Me, too," I replied. "But I have some things I need to do this weekend."

I waved to them as they pulled out of the driveway.

I cleaned the kitchen and found Nikki sitting out on the back deck. She seemed surprised to see me.

"I thought we should talk," I said to her.

"Yes, we should," she answered.

"Listen, Nikki..."

"John?"

"Yes?"

"John, I'm pregnant."

"That's not funny, Nikki."

"Do you see me laughing?"

She pulled up the over-sized t-shirt she had on. She was already showing.

"How?" I asked her. "I don't understand."

"The last time we were together...I'm a little over four months."

"But you are taking birth control pills, Nikki."

She looked at me and then slowly lowered her eyes. "No, I haven't been taking them for awhile now."

I could feel all the color leave my face. I started to pace. I looked again at her stomach and then at her face. "You stopped taking your birth control pills? You stopped taking them without telling me? What in the world were you thinking?"

She answered softly and with no emotion in her voice. "I didn't see the harm. We had not been intimate in awhile. I didn't think it was such a big deal."

"You didn't think it was such a big deal? Did I hear you right? I don't believe this," I said shaking my head. "I can't deal with this right now. I have to go."

I got in my truck and left. I felt sick on my stomach. I pulled over on the side of the road and started beating my fist against the dash board.

No! No!! No!!! This can't be happening! Not now!!

Oh Brooke...my sweet Brooke. She will be waiting to hear from me. She will be wondering how Nikki took the news about the divorce.

I can't talk to her right now. She will know something is wrong as soon as she hears my voice.

I just need some time. Yes, I just need some time to think. This doesn't change anything. This doesn't change how I feel.

Oh man, what am I going to do?

I rode around until after dark. I needed to talk to someone. I drove over to Rick's. Linda met me at the front door.

"Come in, John. Rick told me the good news. Congratulations. I know she's a wonderful lady."

Linda looked at the expression on my face and realized something was wrong. "What is it, John? What's wrong?"

I just stood there shaking my head.

Linda grabbed my arm and walked me in the house. Rick was sitting in the den watching television. He got up and walked over to me. "What's wrong?" he asked.

"Sit down, John. Talk to us," Linda said. I sat down on the couch and she and Rick sat down beside me.

I told them I had just been to talk to Nikki about getting a divorce, but she had hit me with her news first.

"Nikki is pregnant."

Rick and Linda sat with their mouths dropped wide open. "Pregnant!" they both said at the same time.

I told them that we hadn't been together more than twice in the past year and that Nikki had taken it upon herself to quit taking her birth control pills.

"We were together the last time about four months ago. That was just a few weeks before I left home."

Linda suddenly jumped up off the couch. "I can't believe she did this," she said. "That woman is a piece of work."

"She had some help, I guess," I said.

"John, she's done it again."

"Done what, Linda?" I wondered what her statement meant.

Linda told me to think back to when Nikki had suggested that we have a second baby. "You remember, John, you were having problems and you had just asked Nikki if she wanted out of the marriage."

Linda continued. "She knows how you feel about your children. She sensed you were getting ready to leave her, John. She knew that getting pregnant was the one way she could keep you from leaving. She didn't quit those pills because she forgot them or thought it wasn't a big deal. This was all well planned, I can assure you. A woman knows when she is most likely to get pregnant."

I sat there in silence. I thought about what Linda had said. I had no way of knowing whether her theory was right or not. I just knew that things were in a big mess.

I looked at my watch. It was getting late. "I need to go. Brooke will be expecting my call."

Rick walked outside with me. "I don't know what to say," he said. "I am so sorry, John."

I looked at Rick. "Man, I don't know what in the world I am going to do."

Rick asked me how Nikki felt about having another baby.

"Who knows? I didn't stick around to find out. I was so shocked when she hit me with the news; I got out of there as fast as I possibly could. I was in no shape to have a rational conversation with her about it."

I continued to shake my head back and forth. "I feel like I'm dying inside, Rick. Brooke is sitting at home right now expecting my call. She is thinking that we can now start to plan our lives together. And instead, I have to tell her that I'm going to be a father again.

"I feel sick. I'm going to turn her whole world upside down. I am going to hurt her so bad."

I thought about Linda's reaction to Nikki being pregnant as I drove to the office. *Oh man, John, how insensitive can you be?*

Linda had tried for years to have a baby and hadn't been able to conceive. I had gone marching in over there and announced that without any concerted effort, Nikki was pregnant again. It all made sense now. I felt terrible that I had reminded both Rick and Linda of such a painful part of their lives.

My thoughts turned to Brooke. This seemed to be my day for hurting the people I loved most.

I could feel my stomach burning as I walked in the office and picked up the phone. I dialed her number.

"Hello?"

"Hi Brooke, it's me."

"I'm so glad to hear from you, John."

As always, hearing her sweet voice on the other end of the line was calming.

"How are you doing, Angel?" I asked.

"John, something is wrong. I can hear it in your voice. Did things not go well with Nikki?"

I swallowed hard. I would have given anything not to have to tell Brooke about the pregnancy, but there was no way around it. She sat quietly and listened as I told her about my conversation with Nikki earlier that day.

"Oh Brooke, I feel so bad. I am so sorry. When I left the house, I drove around just trying to make sense of it all."

"And have you been able to make sense of it all?" she asked.

"No, Sweetheart, there is no making sense of this. Things are in a big mess here and I've never been so confused in my life about what I am supposed to do. I am so sorry."

I didn't know what to expect from Brooke. I knew that she had every right to tell me that she didn't want to hear from me again. But she didn't do that.

Her voice was tender and reassuring. "Please don't apologize to me, John. You have been honest with me from the start about your situation at home. I'm a big girl. I went into our relationship with my eyes wide open. I love you! And not just in the good times."

"I love you, too, Brooke." I knew she could hear the sadness in my voice.

There was a long silence on the phone. I had never been at a loss for words with her, but I didn't know what to say.

Brooke finally broke the silence. "John, we have always been open and honest with each other about everything. That is one of the things that has made our relationship so special. Please don't shut me out now."

"Oh Brooke, I don't want to shut you out. But I have hurt you so bad and I don't want to say or do anything to hurt you further."

Brooke's voice was still soft and sweet, but now firm. "Yes, I am disappointed that this didn't go as planned, and yes, I am hurting right now, but it is what it is. And now it has to be dealt with."

I managed a slight smile. "Now you sound like my dad. He always said you have to play the cards you are dealt."

"Exactly," she said.

"Man, I wish we hadn't been dealt such a lousy hand."

Brooke laughed. It felt good to hear her laugh. "Now, that's the John I know and love." She always managed to find a way to make me feel better, no matter what the situation.

"Now you listen to me, John David Hughes. I do love you. And I'm not about to turn my back on you when you need me most. I hope you know me well enough to know that. And more than anything else, you need a friend right now. Please let me be there for you."

I began to cry. "What did I ever do to deserve someone like you?"

"That works both ways, you know," she said. "John, you are exhausted. I can hear it in your voice. Please try to get some rest, and we will talk again tomorrow."

Brooke and I said goodnight. She was right...I was exhausted. I lay down and went to sleep.

Brooke and I continued to spend a lot of time together on the phone over the next few weeks. She stuck by me just as she said she would. She was supportive and listened to me whenever I needed to talk. She was my rock.

We grew even closer, and if possible, I loved her even more. I wanted to be selfish. I wanted to turn my back on my responsibilities and continue to make plans for our future.

"What am I going to do, Brooke?" I asked her.

"You are the only one who can answer that, John," she said. "We all have to do what is right. We have to be able to look ourselves in the mirror each morning and be proud of the person looking back at us."

I thought about how I had felt about Ben's father when I found out he had walked out on the woman carrying his child and his baby.

There was no way I could think of divorcing Nikki while she was carrying my child. And no matter what problems we had, or how much resentment I carried because of the circumstances of the pregnancy, the fact remained that I had a child on the way. And that child was innocent and didn't deserve to be caught in the middle of the mess I was in. That child deserved to have me in his or her life just as much as David and Chris had.

"John, do you remember when you told me that your life was filled with ironies?" Brooke asked as we talked that next night.

"Yes, I remember," I answered.

"Well, how about this for irony? One of the reasons I love you so much is because you are such a good father and you love your family so much. And that is the very reason that we both know you can't leave them and come to be with me."

She continued. "You know, I could live with myself if you left Nikki to be with me. She doesn't deserve a good man like you. But I could never live with myself if I took you away from your children."

I tried to speak, but couldn't. My heart felt like it was being torn into little pieces.

We both knew in our hearts what we had to do.

I could hear her quietly crying on the other end of the line. "John, I know you have to go home. But will you please do something for me first?"

"Anything, Sweetheart," I said.

"I want to see you one last time before you do."

Dad, Please Come Home

Brooke was standing at the Atlanta airport waiting for me when I got off the plane. It had been a couple of months since I had gone to ask Nikki for a divorce and had gotten the news of the pregnancy instead.

She was standing there with her arms outstretched and a big smile on her face, but I could see the sadness in her beautiful green eyes. I walked briskly to her and hugged her, wrapping my arms tightly around her. It felt good and familiar being with her again. It felt right. This wonderful girl from South Carolina was the one I was meant to be with. I was convinced of it. But I knew it was not to be.

We drove to a restaurant and found a quiet spot in the corner to sit and talk. I looked at my sweet Brooke. I marveled at her beauty and the warmth of her smile. I was with the one who knew and understood me and who loved me in spite of all my faults...the one I had been dreaming of my whole life...the one I loved.

"Talk to me, John. Tell me everything you are feeling. I want to know."

I leaned over the table and touched the gold necklace hanging around her neck. I held the angel in my hand.

"It's not fair. I want your beautiful face to be the first thing I see each morning when I wake up and the last thing I see each night before I go to sleep. I want to come home every day with a smile on my face because I know I am coming home to you. I want to be with you and grow old with you, Brooke."

I let go of the gold angel and watched as it fell next to her heart. I took her hand. "Why is this happening?" I asked.

Brooke looked down at my hand as I reached for hers. "I don't know," she said sadly. "But I will tell you what I do know. I know what a fine man you are. And I know we have to do what's right or it will continue to eat away at you and destroy you.

"I want us to be together, too, John. I've never wanted anything so bad in my life. But I want us to be together only if it's right. I don't want you to look at me one day and resent me for taking you away from your family. I want you to always feel good about us; to always have a smile on your face when you think about me."

Brooke's eyes met mine. "I have something I need to tell you," she said cautiously.

"What?" I asked, looking anxious.

"Gregory's time in the service is up soon. He will be coming home."

"When?" I asked.

"In about three months. Ironically, about the time your baby is due."

Brooke continued to talk, her eyes never leaving mine. "John, he wants to marry me when he gets home."

I felt like I had just taken a heavy blow to the stomach. "What did you tell him?" I asked.

"I told him we would talk when he gets home."

"Brooke, I am going to ask you something, and I want you to be honest with me, okay?"

"I will never be anything but honest with you, John."

"Do you love Gregory?"

"Yes, I love Gregory," she answered. "But I am not in love with him, John. I am in love with you. Tell me not to marry him...to wait on you...that we can one day be together."

Tears were filling my eyes. My heart felt like it was being ripped out of my chest.

"Sweetheart, you can't imagine how bad I want to tell you not to marry him...to wait on me until I can be with you. But I can't. I'm not in a position to tell you that."

I slowly leaned over to her and kissed her. "You deserve to be happy, Brooke. You deserve to have a husband and Ben deserves to have a father."

I found myself wanting to be selfish and to tell her not to marry Gregory and to wait on me. But I couldn't.

The food came to the table, but neither of us could eat. We went to the hotel and checked into our room.

Brooke had asked me to bring some pictures of my family and she did the same. We got them out and spread them on the bed. She looked at the pictures of David and Chris. "What handsome boys you have!" she said. "David looks just like his dad. And I can see the mischief all over Chris's face," she said, now smiling.

There was a picture of me when I was a little boy. She loved the picture and asked if she could have it. I told her to take what she wanted, and she chose that picture and a couple of me with the boys.

I looked at the ones she had brought. Ben was a cute little guy with his mom's green eyes and smile. I saw a picture of her mom and then a beautiful picture of Brooke that she said had been taken just a few weeks earlier.

"Is it okay if I have this one?" I asked.

"Sure," she said. She got a pencil off the nightstand and wrote 'Brooke' on the back and handed it to me. "I don't want you to forget my name," she said, trying to smile but with tears in her eyes.

I took her into my arms and kissed her. "Oh, Angel, there is no way I could ever forget you. You will always be with me, even when we are apart."

We moved the pictures off the bed and lay down beside each other. I kissed her and pulled her close. She closed her eyes as I ran my fingers up and down her back and arms. I wanted to savor each and every moment of our last night together...the smell of her hair...the sweet taste of her kisses...the warmth of her skin against mine...I knew that the memories of this night would have to last a lifetime.

We lay there together, her heart beating against mine, the gold angel pressed tightly between us.

We talked about staying in touch, but both knew it wasn't the right thing to do. Brooke put her head on my chest. She began to second guess our decision. "How am I ever going to be happy without you in my life, John?"

"I don't know, Sweetheart," I said as I stroked her long, silky hair. "I don't know."

She clutched the necklace and held it close to her heart. "I will need to know that you are okay. What's the harm in an occasional phone call?"

I couldn't imagine my life without her. But I knew that under the circumstances, we didn't have any other choice.

"I know what you are saying, Angel, but can't you see? I can't have contact with you and not want to be with you. I would live in constant turmoil. I would be constantly reminded that you are with him and not with me. I can't go back to just being friends, Brooke. I feel far too much for you for that.

"Brooke," I continued softly, "I've always known that Gregory was in the picture, but with him overseas, I have managed for the most part to keep him out of my mind. I don't want to know you as someone else's wife. I couldn't bear that. I want to remember us just like this... just you and me.

"If you are to have a happy marriage, and if I am to go back to my family, then we have to say goodbye. Can't you see, Angel? It's the only way."

Brooke raised her head off my chest and looked deeply into my eyes. "I love you, John David Hughes," she said. "And I will always love you. There is a reason we met, and this isn't the end for us. It can't be. I will never, ever give up hope that someday, somehow we will be together."

I kissed Brooke again and we went to sleep.

When I awoke early the next morning she was gone. There was an envelope on the bed where she had slept next to me with her South Carolina address on it. Inside the envelope was a card with a picture of a cottage by the sea. I opened the card and read the words she had written inside...

I couldn't stay to tell you goodbye, because in my mind, this isn't goodbye for us. I love you, John, and I will NEVER stop believing in someday.

You and me and the cottage by the sea...Be happy, my love...

Brooke

I held the picture in my hands that she had given me the night before and lay on the bed and cried until there were no more tears.

I got dressed and caught my plane back to Montana.

It was time to go home to my family.

"Mr. Hughes, can you hear me?" Dr. Lewis was looking into my eyes with an ophthalmoscope.

Yes, I can hear you. Will you please get that bright light out of my eyes?

David and Chris and Charlie were standing at the end of the bed. Their dad's eyes had remained open...fixed straight ahead in an eerie, blank stare.

"Mr. Hughes, if you can hear me, can you blink your eyes for me?" Dr. Lewis asked.

Dr. Liebovich and Nurse Fulton stood on the other side of the bed as they continued to examine their patient.

Man, I feel weird. Where am I? Who are these people and what do they want?

Think John...try to remember. Yes, it's all coming back to me...the wreck, the hospital...the doctors.

Am I alive? Did I make it? If so, then it's time to wake up.

*Wake up, John. **You made it. Wake up now!***

Charlie walked to the side of the bed. "Dad, it's Charlie. Can you see me?"

My boy...Charlie...Concentrate, John...Try to focus...

"Look Chris...look at Dad's eyes," David said, his voice excited.

They watched closely as his eyes followed Charlie. Dr. Lewis stepped aside so Charlie could get closer to his father. Charlie took his hand.

"Hi Dad, it's me...it's Charlie," he said.

They watched his mouth as a hint of a smile formed on his face. They watched his lips as they slowly started to move. Everyone held their breath as he struggled to speak. The words came out soft and slow and slurred. But everyone heard and understood them.

"Hi~~~~Son,~~~~~I~~~~~~~Lo~~~ve~~~~~You!"

Charlie was crying as he put his arms around his dad.

I looked around the room. My vision was slowly beginning to clear. I tried to raise my head off the pillow.

"Whoa, not so fast, Mr. Hughes," Dr. Liebovich said as he stepped closer to his patient.

"I~~~~wa~~~nt~~~~to~~~get~~~~up!"

I heard crying. I strained to see who was standing at the foot of the bed. I saw David and Chris hanging onto each other and sobbing uncontrollably.

"Da~~~vid,~~~~Chris...~~~~Dad~~~~needs~~~~a~~~~hug."

Nurse Clara Fulton stood back in the corner of the room and witnessed the most emotional moment she had ever experienced. She had watched these past weeks as those three boys had kept a constant vigil beside their father's bed...never giving up on him...never losing their faith.

She was grateful that she was on duty to see this touching scene as a father came back to his sons. She said a silent prayer of thanks for a reunion that was not expected to happen.

She cried as she watched David and Chris join Charlie by the side of their father's bed. She and Dr. Lewis and Dr. Liebovich quietly left the room. They were all wiping tears from their eyes.

Nurse Clara Fulton looked back toward the bed as she exited the room. The Hughes family had a lot of catching up to do. But there was plenty of time for that later. For now, the boys were all leaning over their dad's hospital bed. They were embracing their father and celebrating a life that had been given back to them.

She walked down the hall. "Out of great tragedy can come great joy," she thought. Because of this father and his three sons, her faith had been renewed…in God and in man.

Roses and a Milkshake

A month had passed since the accident. Aunt Marie was standing by the hospital bed once again crying. But this time, the tears were tears of joy.

"You can really go home, John? Oh, I am so thankful."

David stood in the room by Uncle Sid, both of them proudly smiling. They walked closer to Aunt Marie.

"The doctors said his recovery has been amazing. It has only been a week since he opened his eyes. His speech has already returned to normal and he's now able to eat solid food again. He is getting stronger every day. He walked all the way down the hall this morning, didn't you, Dad?"

"Yes, I did. And Aunt Marie, thanks to you and Uncle Sid offering to stay at the house with me for awhile, the doctors said they could see no reason to keep me here any longer."

Uncle Sid spoke up. "Now, John, you know we wouldn't have it any other way. I can't tell you how happy this makes me."

"They have run all kinds of tests and don't see any evidence of any long-term or short-term memory loss," David said. "The doctors say they don't see any reason that Dad won't make a full recovery."

Aunt Marie started to cry harder. "I have prayed so hard for this day."

David went over and hugged her. "All of our prayers have been answered, Aunt Marie."

The phone rang and David answered it.

"Dad, it's Chris. He is on his way over. He is going to bring some clothes for you to wear home tomorrow, and wants to know if there is anything else he can get for you."

"I can't think of anything," I said. "Wait a minute…yes, tell Chris to go by the florist and pick me up a dozen red roses and bring them with him."

David was laughing. "He wants to know why."

I smiled at David. "Tell your brother that he doesn't have to know everything…just to bring them."

"Well, we have to go," Aunt Marie said. "I am planning a special dinner for tomorrow when you get home. I want all of you boys to be there," she said, looking at David.

Chris came in with the clothes and the roses.

"Thanks, Son. Now, hand me that card and give me a pen, please."

I carefully sat up in bed and started to write. My handwriting was a bit shaky, but it was legible. 'To: Nurse Clara Fulton.'

David and Chris looked at the card and smiled.

"Talk about perfect timing," Chris said as he looked up.

"I see all my favorite guys are here." Nurse Fulton had just come into the room.

"What beautiful roses," she said as she looked over at the table.

"Will you please read the card for me?" I asked, looking over at the boys and winking.

She picked the roses up and read the card. "These are mine?" she asked. "Thank you, Mr. Hughes. This is so nice."

The boys listened as I spoke to Nurse Fulton. "I just wanted you to know how much I appreciate everything. You have taken such good care of me and have been so good to my boys. I will always be grateful."

I motioned for her to come closer and whispered to her. "And when I almost checked out…thanks for reminding me how much I had to live for."

She was surprised. "You heard what I said to you, Mr. Hughes?"

"I heard every single word. And please, my name is John."

Nurse Fulton thanked me again for the roses.

Chris came closer to the bed. "Hey, no secrets," he said. "And you only got roses, Nurse Clara? As many baths as you've given Dad and as much of him as you've seen, don't you think a ring might be more appropriate? Dad, don't you think you should make an honest woman out of this sweet nurse?"

Nurse Fulton was laughing. "Well, Chris, if I wasn't already married, I sure might have to consider that."

She turned back toward me and continued, still laughing. "I told you that I figured this one is a handful. I see that he for sure is."

"Yes, he's been a handful his entire life. And that reminds me," I said, "Christopher, I still owe you one for playing that rap cd while I wasn't able to do anything about it."

Chris grinned mischievously and looked at Nurse Fulton. "Dad was aware of more than we knew."

Nurse Clara looked proudly at her roses. "Yes, I know," she said. "I will never forget you and your fine family, Mr. Hughes...I mean, John."

"And we will never forget you, Nurse Clara. Thank you for everything," they said as she left with her roses.

Rick brought Charlie over later that afternoon.

"Can I stay with you tonight, Dad?" Charlie asked.

"Sure you can. That would be great," I answered.

I looked at David and Chris. "I want you two to go home and get some rest. Tomorrow is a big day."

I asked Charlie to walk down with them as they left. "Will you please go to the cafeteria and get me a vanilla milkshake, Son? Your ole man needs to put some weight on."

I watched as the boys left the room. I wanted to talk to Rick.

Rick walked over to the bed. "So, I hear you are getting to bust out of this joint tomorrow."

"Yes, I am, and I can't wait."

"You had us scared, you know."

"Yes, that's what I've heard. Rick, how do I ever thank you, Man?"

"You listen to me, my old and dear friend," he said. "You can thank me by taking all the time you need to get well and by not worrying about things at the office."

"You know me well," I said.

"Yes, I do. Seriously, John, things are fine with the business. You take all the time you need. It will all be waiting for you when you're ready."

"It is going to be so good to get out of here tomorrow, Rick."

"I know that's true," he said. "John, do you remember everything that happened?" he asked with a serious expression on his face.

"It's all slowly coming back to me in bits and pieces," I answered. "You know, Rick, they say that right before someone dies that their entire life flashes before them. Over the last weeks, mine has seemed to play itself out in slow motion. When I woke up and the doctor was shining a bright light in my eyes, I didn't know if I was dead or alive.

"And if you are wondering if I remember the wreck...yes, I do." There was a long pause. "Rick, did you see the wreck?"

Rick nervously answered. "I didn't see the actual wreck, but I came along soon afterwards. But we can talk about all that another time," he said.

"I just have to know one thing," I said looking up at my best friend. "Did Nikki suffer?"

"No, John, she didn't," Rick answered. "She never knew what hit her."

"Good."

Rick came closer to the bed. He lowered his voice as he spoke. "There is something I need to tell you before Charlie gets back. David has asked about Brooke. He saw her picture in your safe when he was looking for some papers he needed. I told him he would have to ask you about her, but he could tell I knew something, I'm sure of it."

"Yes, he has asked me twice about her that I know of. Both times I heard him, but I wasn't able to respond."

"But that's just it, John. You did respond. David told me that the mention of Brooke's name is what brought you back to us. He's now more curious than ever. What will you tell him when he asks you about her?"

I looked at Rick and thought about what he had said. "I will tell him the truth."

"Do you still think about her, John?"

"Yes, every single day. I wonder how she's doing."

"Are you going to contact her?"

"No."

"You know she would want to know, John."

"I can't do that. She has a family and has moved on. That would be awful selfish of me to go charging back into her life. Besides, it's been a long time. I'm sure she hasn't thought about me in years."

I looked out the window. "I sure hope she's had a good life, Rick.

"Man, thanks for keeping Charlie," I said. "How has he been?"

"It's been hard for him, but he's tough like his dad."

Charlie walked back into the room with my milkshake. "Who is tough like his dad?" he asked.

Rick playfully hit him on the arm. "No one you would know." He smiled. "Okay, you two, I am going to get out of here."

"Aunt Marie is cooking a big welcome home dinner tomorrow," I told him. "I hope you and Linda can make it."

"We wouldn't miss it," Rick said. "Charlie, you keep the ole boy out of trouble tonight."

Charlie grinned and said he would.

Charlie sat and watched as I drank my milkshake and then walked with me to the bathroom. I was able to walk on my own, but was still a little unsteady on my feet. The boys insisted on walking beside me in case I lost my balance and began to fall.

I got back in the bed and Charlie lay down beside me. I smiled as I noticed his feet hanging off the end of the bed. "Good gracious, Son, how much have you grown?" It was amusing to see us both lying in the small hospital bed. Charlie curled up next to me just as he used to do when he was a little boy. I put my arm around him.

"Tell me what it was like, Dad...being in a coma, I mean."

"Well, it's hard to explain, but I will try." I tried to think of a way to help Charlie understand what it had been like for me.

"Charlie, do you remember when we went camping last year, and how thick the fog was early the next morning? It was so thick that we couldn't see our hands in front of our faces."

"Yes, I remember that, Dad," he said.

"Well, it was a little like that. When I first woke up after the accident, I felt like I was in a very thick fog. And I felt confused because I didn't know where I was or where I had been. And I was so tired…more tired than I've ever been in my life.

"I tried to fight my way out of the fog for awhile, but finally decided to just lie down and wait for it to clear. I knew I was hurt real bad, Son, and I almost gave up, but someone came to me and reminded me that you boys loved me and needed me and I had to keep on fighting; that I couldn't give up. So I started to again fight my way through the dense fog.

"There were times I didn't think I was going to make it out, but eventually, I started to see a clearing in the distance. And as the fog began to clear, my mind began to clear, too. And I finally realized that I was going to make it out. That happened to me when I saw you standing by me next to the bed, Charlie. I knew I had made it out and back to you."

Charlie studied my face and thought about what I had said. "Dad, I prayed like I've never prayed before for you to come back to me. And while I was in the Chapel praying, I felt a hand on my shoulder and a man told me not to worry anymore, that you were going to be okay."

"When was this, Charlie?" I asked, curious about what my son had just told me.

"It was the next day after you were brought in. The doctor called us all into a room and told us that you weren't going to make it; that you were hurt too bad. David and Chris and I went to the Chapel to pray for you. The hand and voice were real, Dad. Someone was really there."

I thought about my father's visit that day. "That was your Grandfather Hughes, Son. That was when I was so tired and had almost given up. He was the one who came to tell me to keep fighting; that you boys needed me. He was with me that day and he was with you, too, Son."

We lay there in silence for a long time, each remembering our experience.

"Tell me how you are doing, Son."

"I'm better now, Dad."

"I am so sorry about your mom, Charlie."

Charlie began to quietly cry.

"It's okay." I tried to comfort him. "You know, I lost my mom when I was just about your age. I know it can help to talk about it."

"You don't mind?" he asked.

"Of course not. I miss her, too."

We talked about his mom for a long while.

"Dad, how did you get better after you lost your mom?"

I rubbed Charlie's head. "Everyone deals with loss differently, Son. There is no right or wrong way to grieve. And in time, the pain you are feeling won't hurt quite so bad. You will always love your mom and miss her, but one day you will find that the pain has gone away and instead of feeling the hurt and the loss, you will feel good inside thinking about the good times you had together."

Charlie listened closely as I continued. "Death is a part of life, Charlie. Life goes on and your mom would want you to be happy and to live yours to the fullest. You can honor your mom and her memory by growing up to be the best man you can possibly be. And your mom will always be with you, Son. Right here," I said as I put my hand over Charlie's heart.

"We have a big day ahead," I said. "We had better get some sleep now."

Charlie got out of the bed and stretched out in the recliner next to me.

I thought about Mimi. "Have you and your brothers been to see Mimi?" I asked.

"Yes, Sir," he answered.

"How is she?"

"She's the same," he said sadly. "We didn't tell her about mom."

"I'm sure that's best," I said. "Goodnight, Charlie."

"Dad, you are really getting to go home tomorrow!" Charlie smiled at me and drifted off to sleep.

The Colonel's Deathbed

I had moved back home the day after I got back from seeing Brooke. I had been sleeping upstairs. When Charlie was born, I moved his bed upstairs with me. He was three months old.

I had just gotten to work. The phone rang. "Uh huh," I heard Rick say. He hung up the phone.

"That was Nikki. They have taken the 'Colonel' to the hospital."

"Why?" I asked.

"I don't know. She just said to tell you that she was taking Charlie over to my place so Linda can take care of him."

I got in my truck and started driving to the hospital. When I got there, Nikki and Mimi were in the waiting room.

"What happened?" I asked.

"They have taken him for tests," Mimi said. "He just collapsed in his study," she said. "I called for an ambulance, and they took him out of there kicking and screaming. He didn't want to come."

The doctors came and told us he was in heart failure; that he had pneumonia and was under oxygen.

I called Linda to see how Charlie was doing.

"Smiling away," she said.

I could picture the sweet little smile on his face. "Will you please call Rick and tell him I am going to be here for awhile?"

Linda said that she would and for me to leave Charlie with her for as long as I needed to.

I thanked her.

They got the 'Colonel' settled in his room. We sat and watched him as he slept. I told Nikki and Mimi to go get some coffee and I would stay with him.

His breathing was shallow and his color wasn't good. He opened his eyes and looked at me.

"Hi, Colonel, how are you feeling?" I asked.

"Like hell," he answered. "Where are the girls?"

"They went to get some coffee."

"Good," he said. "I need to talk to you."

I moved closer. "Yes, Colonel?"

His voice was weak. "John, there is something I've wondered about all these years, and I figure if I'm ever going to find out, I'd better ask now."

"What have you wondered, Colonel?"

"All those years ago when I made you that offer…did you ever wish you had taken me up on it and took off?"

"What a question to ask, Colonel!" I said surprised. "The oxygen is getting to the old man's brain," I thought, somewhat amused.

"No, I'm serious," he said. "I know it hasn't been easy; being married to my girl, I mean. Most men would have taken off long ago."

It was apparent that the 'Colonel' had not been aware of our separation, and no purpose would be served by bringing it up now.

I pulled up the nearest chair and sat down by his bed. "Colonel, have you ever heard the story, 'if worms had machine guns'?"

He shook his head and said that he hadn't.

I had never talked to the 'Colonel' about my parents or my life growing up in Illinois. But I sat there and told him about my dad's drug store and the rape trial in our small community all those years ago when I was a boy. And I told him my dad's story of the little man wiping the smirks off the faces of those big shot lawyers in his store that day.

"If worms had machine guns, then birds wouldn't mess with them."

Even as weak as the 'Colonel' was, he managed to laugh long and hard.

"My dad used that story to teach me not to dwell on the 'what ifs' of life, Colonel. What if Nikki had never gotten pregnant? What if I had taken you up on your offer? Life is full of 'what ifs', but in the scheme of things, the 'what ifs' don't mean a thing. What matters is 'what is'.

"And the reality...the 'what is' in my life is that I have a wife and three wonderful boys who I love with all my heart. And no, Colonel, it hasn't always been easy, but nothing in life worthwhile ever is. I have tried to take one day at a time and do the very best I can to be a good father and husband."

I thought about Brooke's words and continued. "I have to be able to look myself in the mirror each morning and feel good about the man looking back at me."

The 'Colonel' was growing weaker and it was hard for him to speak. He motioned for me to lean in closer to him. "John, I want you to know how proud I am to have you for a son-in-law. I know you will take good care of my wife and baby girl when I'm gone."

"Yes, Sir, you know I will always take care of them. But you are going to get well and get out of here, Colonel." I could feel my eyes filling with tears. "And that's an order, Sir."

The 'Colonel' smiled and reached for my hand. "I am dying and I won't be getting out of here, John. But do you have any idea how good it feels to be able to die in peace knowing that my wife and baby girl will be looked after? Thank you, Son."

I turned my head away to wipe the tears. I saw Nikki standing at the door. She was crying, but managed a smile when her eyes met mine.

The 'Colonel' died later that day with Nikki and Mimi and me by his side. He had lived to see the birth of his third grandson.

I told Nikki that I would go over to pick up Charlie, but she insisted on going herself.

There was a beautiful sunset that day as I drove home from the hospital. I thought about Brooke. I wished I could tell her of the 'Colonel's' death and his words to me before he died. She would be proud to know what he had said to me and that he had called me 'Son'.

I wondered if Gregory had made it home and if the wedding day had been set. I wanted to tell her about my sweet little boy, Charlie. I hoped she was doing well. I missed her.

I had thought about it many times through the years and had wondered what it would do to Nikki to lose her dad. I had my doubts that she would be able to deal with it.

Linda later told me of her conversation with Nikki that day when she went to pick up Charlie. She told Nikki how sorry she was that her dad had passed away.

Nikki asked Linda if she would please sing at the 'Colonel's' funeral. "My dad loves to hear you sing in church, Linda. He would like that."

Linda told her she would be honored to sing at his funeral.

Nikki put Charlie in the car and walked back to her and hugged her. "Linda, I owe you a huge apology. You have tried for years to reach out to me and I have been mean to you. I am so sorry and I hope you can forgive me. I would love to be able to start over."

The night after we buried the 'Colonel', Nikki came upstairs where Charlie and I were sleeping. I woke up as she climbed in bed next to me.

She spoke softly. "John, I am ready to be a good wife to you and a good mother to our boys. Will you please give me another chance?"

I picked Charlie up and took him downstairs and started sleeping again in the bed with my wife.

Mimi was diagnosed with Alzheimer's disease soon after she lost her husband. We were finally able to convince her to come live with us. There were good days and bad days, and in time her mind slowly deteriorated and her memories left her. We sadly had to say goodbye to the Mimi we had known as she slipped further away from us.

She eventually needed more care than we were able to provide and we found a nursing home nearby. Nikki had been to see her mom every day since she had been there.

Yes, I had often wondered how Nikki would handle the death of her father. I had my answer. The day the 'Colonel' died was the day my wife finally grew up.

Revelations

His dad had been out of the hospital for a month now and they were having a family cookout. David came over early in hopes of having some time to talk to him.

He pulled up to the house and saw him sitting out on the back deck. David knew something was bothering him. He had heard it earlier in his voice on the phone and he could see it now on his face as he sat looking out into the distance, unaware of his son's presence.

"Hi, Dad."

He jumped, startled that someone was there. "Well, hi Son, I didn't know you were here." He looked around. "Are Jessica and Allison not with you?"

"No," David answered. He pulled up a chair next to his dad. "They're coming over later. Where is everyone?"

"Charlie went with Uncle Sid to check on his place. Aunt Marie is taking a nap. And Chris and Paige will be over in a little while."

"How are you doing, Dad?" David asked.

"I'm fine," he said, answering too quickly. "You should see those huge ribeyes we are going to grill. I hope you are hungry."

"I will be," David assured him.

"Dad, I'm worried about you. Is everything okay? Are you feeling alright? The doctors are giving you good reports on your follow-up visits, aren't they?"

"Yes, Son, I'm getting good reports. I guess it's just going to take some time..."

"What's going to take some time?"

There was a long silence. Then he spoke. "It should have been me, David."

"It should have been you? What do you mean, Dad?"

He then broke down and the words came pouring out. "It should have been me driving that car, David. I always drove when we were together. Why wasn't it me behind the wheel when that kid came crashing in on the driver's side? Why did I even buy that car in the first place? Why couldn't we have stayed at the restaurant just a little while longer? Why did this happen to your mom?"

David listened. His stomach began to hurt as he realized that the guilt was eating his father alive. "But it wasn't supposed to be you, Dad. It was Mom's time, that's why. A time to live and a time to die, remember?"

David continued, "Dad, I miss Mom so much and I know you do, too. But she's gone now and you are still here with us. And it's time for you to get over this guilt. It wasn't your fault, Dad. Mom died knowing you were with her and you loved her.

"You were almost taken from us, too. But thankfully, we had a miracle and we have you with us. And it's time for you to start living again. Dad, do you hear me? It's time."

David watched as his dad got up and walked to the other side of the deck. He then turned and came to him and put his arms tight around him. "Thank you, Son. I feel like a huge weight has been lifted off my shoulders. I needed to hear that.

"Now if I can only convince your little brother that he doesn't have to watch my every move. He has been looking so forward to his basketball camps this summer, but did you know he is saying he's not going? I have tried to tell him I am doing well and will be just fine, but he has it in his head that he doesn't need to go and leave me here alone. I tell you...Charles Brandon is about as stubborn as anyone I've ever seen."

"I can't imagine where he would have gotten that from," David said grinning.

"Nor can I," his father said with a smile on his face.

David was glad to see the familiar smile return to his father's face. "Okay, David, it's now or never," he thought to himself. He stumbled around trying to find the words. "Dad...I need to ask you about something."

"You want to know about Brooke."

His words surprised him. "How in the world did you know that?"

He listened as his dad explained to him that he had heard him ask about her while he was in the hospital.

"I knew you heard me," David said excited. "I knew when I mentioned her name you were trying to respond to me."

"Yes, Son, I heard it all. And first of all, you are more than welcome to read the letter to me from your Grandfather Hughes."

David sat looking at him in amazement. "You aren't kidding that you heard it all. Dad, if you don't feel comfortable talking to me about her, then I will drop it. But you have to know...my curiosity has gotten the better of me. I want to know about this woman whose picture you kept in your safe all these years. I am convinced that Brooke, without even being here, had a big part in bringing you back to us."

He chose his words carefully. "Son, I don't mind telling you anything you might want to know about her. I just don't want you to feel any less toward me and I sure don't want you to feel any disrespect on my part toward your mom."

He looked at David. "This is tough for me. It's hard to admit to your son that you didn't always practice what you preached. Even though your mom and I were separated, I was still a married man and I am not proud of how I handled things."

David understood what he was saying. "Dad, I very well remember how things were back in those days. And I am grown now. I know that things can happen. And I had already figured out that Brooke had probably come into your life while you were separated from Mom."

"Yes, that's true, David," he said. "Brooke was a special angel who I met at a time in my life when I badly needed one."

David sat back and listened as his dad told him about Brooke. He told him about their meeting on the computer and the long-distant connection that they had made.

"We became friends and before I knew it, I had some strong feelings for her. We fell in love, Son. It all happened so fast. We had planned to be together and then I found out your mom was pregnant with Charlie.

"We realized that as much as we loved each other and as much as we wanted to be together, it wasn't meant to be. There were too many people that we loved who would be hurt, and neither of us could have handled that. We knew the right thing to do was to say goodbye and for me to go home to be with my family.

"Then Charlie was born and Grandpa died. You know, Son, I thought your mom would fall completely apart when her dad died, but I was wrong. She finally got it all together. And I owed it to her and to all of you boys to keep our family together.

"And we had some very good years together, didn't we, David?"

"Yes, Dad, we did." He thought of the picture and the girl with the beautiful eyes. "Her green eyes are beautiful, Dad," he said.

"You should see them in person. They are the color of emeralds."

"You loved her."

"Yes, very much."

David looked at his father. He had never seen his eyes brighter or his expression more sure. "You still love her."

"I will always love her. You can't know Brooke and not love her."

David got out of his chair. "Dad, you need to call her. How long since you've talked to her?"

He was surprised to hear that they had not talked in all these years.

"It was the only thing to do, Son. I couldn't live my life like that. It wouldn't have been fair to my family or to hers."

David listened as he told him about Gregory and Ben.

"I have lived my life telling myself that she's been happy and has had a good life. That's all I knew to do."

"So, it's been over fifteen years?" David asked.

"Yes, since right before Charlie was born."

"Then, Dad, you probably wouldn't be able to find her anyway. Do you think she's still living in South Carolina?"

His dad smiled. "Oh yea, she's still living right there where she always lived."

"How can you know that?" he asked.

"She loved that land. It belonged to her father. He was killed in a logging accident when she was a little girl, and that was the land he loved. She may have replaced that little wood frame house she used to live in, but you can bet your bottom dollar if she's in a new house, it's sitting right there on her daddy's land.

"She was quite a special lady, Son. You would have loved her, too."

David and I got the grill going and the whole family gathered later that day for a steak dinner. After the meal I asked for everyone's attention. I could feel the emotion building inside me as I looked around the room at my family. Little Allison was sitting in my lap. I hugged my granddaughter.

I cleared my throat and took a deep breath and began. "This means so much to me having everyone together today. I know that I am here only because of each of you. Because of your faith and your prayers and because you refused to give up on me, we are able to have this time together. And I know that you can all feel Nikki here with us today as I can."

My voice cracked as I continued. "I am so blessed. And I want to thank each of you for everything you've done for me when I couldn't do it for myself. But I have been getting stronger every day, and I can finally truthfully say that I am now able to take care of myself again. And it's now time for you all to get on with your lives.

"David, it's time to quit worrying about your dad and to start concentrating on your family and your career. Chris, you've got a wedding to plan, Son. And Charlie, school is about out, and it's time for you to start packing for basketball camp."

Charlie started shaking his head. "I am not going anywhere this summer, Dad. I'm staying right here with you."

"Well," I answered him, "then you will be here alone. Cause your ole man is leaving for the summer."

Everyone was staring at me. "What do you mean, you are leaving for the summer?" they all asked.

I smiled and said, "David came over earlier today and we talked. He said some things that made me realize that it's time for us to start moving on with our lives. We've all been through a lot and if we have been taught anything, it's that life is short, and it's meant to be lived and enjoyed. Your mom would want that for all of us, right, Charlie?" I said as I winked at him.

"Right, Dad," Charlie said, grinning at me. "Where are you going?"

"Well, I have always thought I would like to spend some time living near the ocean. I am going to check into renting a little cottage on the Oregon coast for the summer."

"But you aren't planning to go alone, are you, Dad?" Chris asked.

"I sure am, Chris. I want you all to listen to me. This is something I feel I need to do. I need this time alone. It will be just the right medicine. When I get home, I will be a new man."

"Dad, I don't know about this," David said hesitantly.

"I understand your concerns, Son. But I need for all of you to please respect my decision and trust me that this is the best thing for me right now. And be happy for me…it's something I've wanted to do for a long time. I'll have to get back to work when I get home. It's now or never. Right, Allison?"

Allison laughed as I took her hands and clapped them together with mine.

"It does sound fun, Dad," Charlie said.

"Does that mean you will start packing for basketball camp now?"

He nodded his head.

"And Christopher and Paige…I assume we will still be having a wedding this fall?"

Chris put his arm around his fiancé. "You had better believe there's going to be a wedding," he said proudly.

I looked over at my aunt and uncle. "Aunt Marie and Uncle Sid… what do I say to you? How do I tell you what you mean to me and how much I appreciate everything? When I lost my mom and dad, you took me in and treated me like your own son. And after the accident, you didn't hesitate to be there for me again. You left your own home to come stay with me until I recovered. I love you both so much. Now it's time to get back to your own place and enjoy all those things you planned to do after retirement."

Aunt Marie was crying again. "Oh John, we have been doing just what we wanted to do."

I smiled at her. "I know you have, Aunt Marie.

"You know, they say what doesn't kill us makes us stronger. I figure if that's true, then we must be one mighty tough bunch."

Everyone was laughing. I looked around the room at each one of them. 'A time to laugh and a time to cry.' There had been far too many tears. David was right. It was time to enjoy life again.

I was excited about my summer plans.

Yes, it's time to move on.

A Trip to South Carolina

David walked into his dad's and Rick's office.

"Hi, David," Rick said, looking up from his desk.

"Hi Rick. How are you doing?"

"I'm fine. Have you talked to your dad?" he asked.

"Yes," David answered, "just this morning. He says he's doing good…that he misses all of us, but this summer vacation is just what he needed."

"He told me the same thing when I talked to him last week," Rick said. "I told him just to make sure he doesn't get too attached to that place. Man, I miss him around here."

David smiled. "Yea, I miss him, too. He sounds good. He said he has put all his weight back on and that he's in the best shape of his life. I can't wait to see him. He should be home in about three weeks."

David cleared his throat and continued. "I came by to get something out of Dad's safe. There's a letter in there written to him from Grandfather Hughes, and Dad said it would be okay if I read it."

Rick got the key out of his desk drawer and went over to the safe and unlocked and opened it. David reached inside and went through the stack of papers until he found the letter. He opened his briefcase and put the letter inside.

He hadn't told Rick the whole truth. He hadn't told anyone what was on his mind. The truth was he wanted something else out of that safe. He reached for the envelope at the bottom of the stack of papers and put it inside his briefcase with the letter.

It was still very early in the morning. The sun had not yet risen over the eastern Montana sky. David boarded the plane, found his seat, and went back to sleep.

He awoke as the drink tray came rattling down the aisle. He took a can of orange juice and a bottle of water. He smiled at the stewardess and thanked her.

David opened his briefcase and found the letter written to his father from his Grandfather Hughes. He looked closely at the piece of paper in his hands. He examined his grandfather's handwriting. It was obvious that the letter had been opened and folded back many times over the years.

He began to read…

Hi Son,

It's your dad. I am writing this to you on the eve of your 13th birthday. My boy has grown up so fast.

I don't know what I did to deserve having such a special boy for my son, but I thank God each and every day for you. I am so proud of you, John, and so proud to have you carry on my name.

You are kind and loving and compassionate, yet strong. You are intelligent and independent. You have always shown total respect to your mother and me. You have a good heart, Son, and that trait is more valuable than a room full of gold.

The world is yours, my boy. You can do whatever it is that your heart desires.

I wish for you a lifetime of happiness and success and love in your life. And I wish for you a son someday who will bring as much joy and happiness into your life as you have brought into mine.

I love you, Son.
Dad

David noticed that the letter was tear-stained. He wondered if the tears were from his grandfather as he had written it or from his father as he had read it. He imagined from both.

He leaned back in his seat. He had not taken a trip to the southeastern part of the country since he and his family had gone to the family reunion in Georgia all those years ago.

He carefully folded the letter and put it back into his briefcase. He then reached for the envelope and looked at the South Carolina address on the front. He pulled Brooke's picture out and studied her face. He wondered if she would still be at that same address as his dad had said she would. He felt something else inside the envelope. There was a card inside that he had not noticed before. There on the front of the card was a picture of a beach house on the ocean. He opened it and read the words written inside...

I couldn't stay to tell you goodbye, because in my mind, this isn't goodbye for us. I love you, John, and I will NEVER stop believing in someday.

You and me and the cottage by the sea...Be happy, my love...

Brooke

Brooke had gotten up later than usual this morning. She had not been sleeping well lately and the night before had been especially restless.

Ben had joined the army and was away at basic training. His dad's death had been extremely hard on him, and in spite of her protests, he wanted to follow in his dad's footsteps and serve his country.

Brooke was alone. She didn't feel good and thought of going back to bed, but she got up and showered and began to get dressed.

Her marriage to Gregory had been good for Ben. He had been the father to him that she had so desperately wanted him to have, and she had appreciated him adopting Ben and raising him as if he were his own son. She had tried to be the best wife she could possibly be.

They had married soon after he returned home from overseas and he had become a fireman. He had been good to them and had given them a good life, and she loved him for that.

She thought back to the morning a couple of years earlier when he had been called out to a fire. There had been a knock on the door a couple of hours later, and when she had seen Gregory's best friend and fellow firefighter standing there and the expression on his face, she knew.

They had already gotten four children out of the burning house. Gregory had gone back inside after a neighbor told him that one of the children who lived there was not accounted for. The little boy had been staying with relatives and was not inside after all. Gregory did not make it out alive.

She thought of her son. She prayed that God would look out for him.

She put on a green blouse and clutched the angel on her necklace that had been given to her so many years ago. At that moment, a jet touched down in South Carolina.

It was a hot, humid summer day. Brooke poured herself a glass of iced tea and got a broom. She went out on the front porch and began to sweep.

She watched as a car turned and began to come up her drive. She put the broom down and reached for the glass of tea. A man got out of the car and began to walk toward her. He was wearing jeans and a white Oxford cloth buttoned-down shirt. Her body suddenly froze as he got closer and the glass fell from her hand and broke on the concrete below.

She didn't move but continued to stare in disbelief as he hurried toward her and bent over to pick up the glass.

"Don't cut your hand," she finally managed to say as she bent over to help him pick up the broken glass.

He looked up and their eyes met. "Are you Brooke?" he asked, already knowing the answer. She had not aged much at all. Her hair was shorter, but she still looked very much the same. And those eyes... Dad was right...they were like emeralds.

"Yes," she said. "I am Brooke."

He stuck his hand out. "It's nice to meet you, Brooke. I am…"

"David," she said, before he had a chance to finish. She reached for him and hugged him. "Oh, David, I am so glad to meet you, too."

She released him and stepped back. "John…is John okay?" There was panic in her voice.

"Yes," David assured her. "He's fine."

Brooke let out a sigh of relief. "So, you know about me. Does John know you are here? How did you find me? Are you sure everything is okay?"

David smiled. He handed her the envelope that she had written her address on all those years ago. He looked at the new house that had been built on the family land just as his father had said it would be.

"Where are my manners? Come inside out of this heat," she said as she opened the door and led the way inside. They walked to the kitchen and she asked David to please sit down at the kitchen table. She poured a glass of tea and handed it to him.

Brooke sat down at the table with him. "You always did look just like your father." She got up and went into her bedroom and brought back the pictures she had of him and Chris and their dad. "You are just about the age John was when we met, you know. When I saw you walking toward me, I couldn't believe what I was seeing.

"Please tell me everything, David. I want to know how everyone is doing."

David told her that he was an attorney; that he had a wife and a little girl named Allison.

"Oh, what a pretty name," she said, smiling. "I bet that little girl has John wrapped around her little finger."

"Of course," he said.

"You know, David, I have never seen a father as proud of his boys as John was of you and your brother. Tell me about Chris."

He told her that Chris was doing fine and was engaged to be married in the fall.

"And what did you have…a little brother or a little sister?"

"Another little brother," David answered. "His name is Charlie." He took his wallet out of his pocket and pulled out a picture of Charlie and Chris.

"What handsome boys!" she said.

David started to put his wallet back in his pocket.

"David, do you happen to have a picture of your dad in there?"

David pulled out a picture of his dad and handed it to Brooke. He sat and watched her face as she looked at it. She tried to hold back the tears, but began to cry. "I have missed him so bad," she said. "The years have been good to him. He is even more handsome than he was the day I met him."

It was apparent to David why his dad had been so attracted to her. She was warm and sweet and sincere. He was comfortable being around her. And it was obvious that she had loved his father very much and still did.

"How is your mom?" she asked.

David sat in silence. She asked again. "How is Nikki?"

David looked down. "Mom is gone," he said.

"Gone? What do you mean, David?" she asked.

David told Brooke all about the birthday and the car and the accident that had taken his mother's life.

"Oh, David, I am so sorry," she said.

David could again hear panic in Brooke's voice. "Was John in the accident?" She anxiously looked at him while she waited for his answer.

"Yes, but he's alright now." David then began telling her the whole story…about the wreck…his mom's death…his dad's coma…their miracle…how hard he had fought to come back to them.

Brooke began to shake. David reached for her hand. "Dad is really alright, I promise."

David then told Brooke how he had come to know about their relationship. He told her about the safe and how he had found the envelope with her address and picture inside when he was looking for his parents' legal papers after the accident.

"When Dad got better, I asked him about you, and he told me. I hope you don't mind me coming. I was curious to meet you."

"And your dad doesn't know you are here?" she asked.

"No," David answered. "No one knows."

"David, why did John not come to me himself?" she asked with a puzzled look on her face.

"I asked him that," David said. "Dad has never stopped loving you, Brooke, and he said he has thought about you and missed you every single day of his life. But he said you were married and had a family and he would never do anything to upset your life."

David looked down and shook his head. "Look, I'm sorry...I shouldn't have said that. I know you have a husband and a family. Dad said he couldn't disrupt your life, and here I am telling you this. He would be very upset with me if he knew I was here."

David looked back again at her. "The last thing I want to do is to disrupt your life. But I love my dad and he has been through so much. And I couldn't quit thinking about you and how you were there for him at a time when he badly needed someone. I hope you understand. I had to meet you."

Brooke got up out of her chair and came over to David and hugged him again. "I am glad you came, David. This means more to me than you will ever know."

She then left the kitchen again and came back with a framed picture of Gregory. "This is my husband. He was a fireman and died two years ago while fighting a house fire."

David looked at the picture of the man in uniform. He had kind eyes.

She then showed him another picture. "And this is my son, Ben. He has joined the army and is in basic training.

"I understand," she said. "Why John didn't contact me, I mean. I did the same thing for the same reasons. I didn't want to cause any problems for your dad or his family."

David smiled. They both loved each other so much until they were willing to sacrifice their own happiness to protect each other.

"You have the most special Dad, David."

"I know," David said. "He gave up everything for us and I love him for it. We needed him, Brooke. Mom needed him. But now, he needs you."

David looked at his watch. "Oh man, I have to go. I have a flight to catch."

David took a business card out of his wallet. He wrote down an Oregon address on the back. "My dad is spending the summer on the Pacific Northwest coast. He rented a cottage on an Oregon bay."

"He's writing his book," Brooke whispered with a big grin on her face.

"What?" David asked.

"Nothing," Brooke said. "I was just thinking...I'm glad he's finally getting to live out his dream."

David took the card out of the envelope and handed it to Brooke. Brooke looked at it and felt all warm inside. "He kept it all these years." She read the words she had written the last time she had seen him...'I will NEVER stop believing in someday...You and me and the cottage by the sea.'

David handed her the business card. "This is where my dad is staying. Don't you think it's finally 'someday'?"

David smiled and walked away.

Brooke watched and waved to him as he got into the car and drove off.

"Yes," she said quietly to herself. "It's finally someday."

A Cottage by the Sea

I poured a cup of coffee and went to sit outside in the rocking chair on the front porch of my cottage. I was feeling well and my strength had returned. The morning jogs on the beach had improved my stamina. The sea air had cleared my head.

I looked out across the vast ocean. It was going to be a good day. I wanted to get some writing done on my book.

Mrs. Roper, an elderly lady renting the cottage next to mine, walked up to the foot of the steps and waved. "Good morning, John."

I waved back. "Good morning, Mrs. Roper."

She and her husband had been married for forty-eight years. She loved the ocean and he loved the mountains. "You have to do your own thing," she told me. "That's the key to longevity in marriage." She spent her summers here on the Oregon Coast and he spent his in the mountains of Yellowstone.

"I'm going into town," she said. "Do you need anything?"

"No, thank you. I have everything I need," I answered.

"By the way, how's the writing coming, John?" she asked.

"I'm just about finished with the book, Mrs. Roper. I just have to decide how it's going to end."

"What's the name of this book, anyway?" she asked.

"If Worms Had Machine Guns."

She turned to walk away and then back toward me again. "That's a strange name for a book," she said as she waved goodbye and continued on her way.

"Yes, but it's been a strange life," I thought as I watched her walk away.

Late that afternoon, I took a long walk on the beach. When I got back to my cottage, I stretched out in the reclining beach chair in the sand next to the water. I listened to the waves as they began to roll ashore.

I covered my face with the newspaper I had been reading and fell into a light sleep.

"Hey, what's a girl got to do to get some attention around here?"

I smiled. I would know that voice anywhere. I loved dreaming about her.

I felt a hand on my leg. "You didn't think you were going to get to enjoy this place all by yourself, did you?"

I opened my eyes. Those beautiful, green emerald eyes were looking into mine. I jumped up out of the chair.

"Brooke...Brooke, is it really you?"

"Yes, John, it's really me." She laughed as I grabbed her and took her into my arms. I held on tight. I was not about to let go. I could feel my heart pounding in my chest.

"How did you know I was here, Sweetheart?" I asked her excitedly.

"Let's just say that you have a son who loves you very much."

"David...he called you?" I asked.

"No, John, he came to see me. It was so good to meet him."

I tenderly kissed her and looked deep into her eyes. "I can't believe you are really here. I love you, Angel. I never stopped loving you."

Her voice was soft and tender. "I love you, too, John. I never stopped believing in someday."

She looked at me. She gently traced the scar on the right side of my face with the edge of her hand. It had healed well and was now barely visible.

"You look good, John. I didn't know what to expect. You have been through so much." She then began to cry. "I am so sorry. I am so sorry about Nikki."

I held her again and ran my fingers through her hair. "It's okay, Sweetheart. It's all over now. Everything is going to be alright."

"Oh, Angel," I said softly, "I have dreamed about this every day since we had to say goodbye. I have missed you so much. You are as beautiful as you were the day I met you."

I kissed her again. "I want to know about your life," I said to her. "I want to know everything."

At that moment, the sun began to set over the water. "Shhh," she said, gently placing her finger on my lips. "We have the rest of our lives to catch up."

She sat down in the beach chair. "Just sit here beside me, John, and enjoy this beautiful sunset with me. I don't want to ever see another one without you."

We watched together as the sun set over the Pacific Ocean. We then walked hand in hand up to the cottage. We talked and laughed and held each other into the early hours of the morning. The years we had been apart disappeared as we picked up where we had left off.

I watched my sweet Brooke's beautiful face as she smiled at me and as her eyes slowly began to close. She fell asleep in my arms.

The sun would soon cast its light on a new day. I quietly got out of bed so I wouldn't wake her. I walked over to the little table by the front window of the cottage and turned on my laptop and began to type. I finally knew how my book would end…